Shoo-Fly Girl

Other Books by Lois Lenski

Autobiographical

A LITTLE GIRL OF NINETEEN HUNDRED

Historical

PHEBE FAIRCHILD, HER BOOK
A-GOING TO THE WESTWARD
BOUND GIRL OF COBBLE HILL
OCEAN-BORN MARY
INDIAN CAPTIVE
BLUEBERRY CORNERS
PURITAN ADVENTURE

Regional

BAYOU SUZETTE
STRAWBERRY GIRL
BLUE RIDGE BILLY
JUDY'S JOURNEY
BOOM TOWN BOY
COTTON IN MY SACK
TEXAS TOMBOY
PRAIRIE SCHOOL
MAMA HATTIE'S GIRL
CORN FARM BOY
SAN FRANCISCO BOY
FLOOD FRIDAY
HOUSEBOAT GIRL
COAL CAMP GIRL

To
my beloved
Amish children

Shoo-Fly Girl

by

Lois Lenski

J.B. Lippincott Company

PHILADELPHIA · NEW YORK

The author thanks Alfred A. Knopf, Inc. for permission to quote from "Sunday
Morning," a poem by Wallace Stevens appearing in *The Collected Poems of Wallace
Stevens.*

CONTENTS

FOREWORD   ix

The World Is Small and Safe
    I   THE FAMILIAR PATH   4
    II A STEP TO ONE SIDE   24

The World Has Open Arms
    III THE HEART'S BURDEN   44
    IV A GODLY CHILD   63

The World Is Fear and Danger
    V   VENTURE INTO THE UNKNOWN   82
    VI CITY OF STRANGERS   97

The World Turns Upside Down
    VII THE GIFT REJECTED   112
    VIII DISASTER FALLS   127

The World Is Peace and Love
    IX DOUBLE TROUBLE   146
    X   NEW-FOUND TREASURE   162

Foreword

In September 1962 a long-cherished dream of mine came true. I found myself in the heart of the Amish country in Lancaster County, Pennsylvania. I had a comfortable place to stay in the home of a Mennonite family, and a rented car, with unlimited time at my disposal. I wanted to get acquainted with the Amish people.

I was told that it would be difficult, but upon my first visit to a one-room Amish school, a door opened for me. After that, more doors opened one by one. Amish friends took me into their homes and made me welcome. I visited in many homes, but to one I returned over and over, for I was made to feel there that I was a part of the family. There were nine children and I shared in their activities and those of their parents, aunts and uncles and grandparents. I drank "meadow tea" with them, I ate at the long table in the kitchen, I asked many questions that were freely answered. I rode in an Amish buggy, I went to House Amish church, I slept in an Amish home and I witnessed a barn-raising. I visited a number of one-room Amish schools, returning to two of them repeatedly. Both teachers and pupils made me welcome.

I am grateful to my Amish friends for making these privileges possible. They knew my purpose and it was their desire that Amish life be depicted in my book as authentically as possible. Without their help, this book could not have been written. My sincere thanks go to Sara E. Fisher, Elmina Stoltzfus, Naomi Lantz, the Fisher family and another Amish family who wish to remain anonymous, and to two non-Amish friends, Ruth Williams and Helen Miller. If this book has any of the true Amish spirit, it is because they helped put it there.

In many ways, this experience has been richer for me than the gather-

ing of material for some previous Regionals books. It became a "labor of love" filled with nostalgia, bringing back to me vivid memories of my own Ohio childhood, so similar in many respects.

It was like opening a door into the past to live with the Amish people, like going back to a way of life that is forever gone and lives only in the memory. But there it was, alive and vigorous, with many whole-hearted participants sharing in it and believing in it. They are living much the same life that small town and rural people in Ohio and Pennsylvania lived in the early 1900s before the advent of the automobile. They have stood still for sixty years and have not moved along with the rest of the world.

In a German, non-Amish community in Ohio, I had had identical experiences and impressions—the kerosene lamps, the wood range in the kitchen and its welcome warmth on a chilly evening, the cold barn at evening lighted by dim lanterns, the milking of cows amid the smell of hay and dust, the Saturday scrubbing of the linoleum kitchen floor on hands and knees, the Saturday baking and getting ready of the children's Sunday clothes, the emphasis of religion of Sunday . . . All these things I had seen and felt and known as a child.

The ride in a buggy behind a horse, the slapping of the lines, the horsy smell, the clop-clop *of the horses' hoofs heard when one is lying in bed at night, the enveloping darkness in the kitchen growing ever darker just before the lamp is lighted, the welcome glow of light shining on little upturned faces, the dark scary shadows in the corners and in stairs and hallways. All these things I saw and sensed and felt as a child. I was also surprised to hear certain words and phrases which were once a part of the warp and woof of my daily life, expressions I had not heard for over fifty years, which are not necessarily Amish but a heritage from early German-Americans. These scenes and these words made me feel very close to the Amish people.*

Then, too, certain aspects of Amish life took me back to early Puritan days. I recalled vividly the research for my book Puritan Adventure, *in primary Puritan sources, diaries, letters, etc. There are many similarities —the large families (the average number of children in an Amish family is nine, some having as many as fourteen or eighteen), the hard work of the children, the strict religious atmosphere based on a fundamentalist interpretation of the Bible, the adult dominance and disregard of the child's own point of view and rights, and the primitive "down-to-earth" practical considerations in daily living. There is one major difference. Amish children are happier and get more joy out of life than Puritan children, so strictly repressed, ever did.*

One evening as I sat at the long lamplit table and looked at the double row of little heads of the children bowed in prayer, sitting close together on the side benches, with Father at the head and Mother at the end of the left bench next to him, I was deeply moved. I was transported in spirit back to the Massachusetts Bay Colony in the 1640s. The only foreign element was the Pennsylvania Dutch speech.

The Amish call themselves "the plain people." It is their desire to dress plain, to eat plain, to live plain. The phrase is singularly appropriate. They wish to live in their own way and to be let alone. They shun all publicity and attention.

One can only admire their stern self-denial in rejecting the ways of the world and feel their modest pride too, when they say quietly, "This is our way. We are Amish." The casual outsider, the average American who is constantly absorbed in "getting," can only conclude that there must be many broken hearts among them and many frustrated souls among the apparently contented majority. Outsiders often feel sorry for the Amish children. But if one studies the faces of children and adults and listens to their words, one can see in them an almost universal peace and contentment, a kind of beauty uncommon among more worldly people. There is no doubt that those who live close to God show it in their faces.

The Amish people have escaped many evils of present-day society by not admitting the machine into their lives, and by getting their living by their own hands from the soil. This has simplified their life and kept them away from commercialism. They take up no collection at church because they have no church expenses to meet. A collection is taken once a month for the welfare of Amish members who cannot care for themselves. Children take loving care of their parents in old age. The Amish refuse Social Security, they carry no insurance. Their wants are few, and they escape the evils of pressure advertising (no radio, television and often no newspaper), the evils of commercialism and political wrangling. They have made a good life for themselves without all the "things" that are now considered an essential part of American life.

And yet there is something incongruous about preserving a vanished way of life in this modern age, something strange about this hanging onto the way of life of their fathers, because it means a stagnant desire for no change, a forcing of contentment in a narrow circle where no change is possible, because it is not allowed. Under the wearing of chains, they dare to be free.

I enjoyed the Amish children thoroughly. Probably no other group of children in America lives as circumscribed and controlled a life as the Amish children do. Yet the effect of this control upon them is amazing. For the most part they live cheerfully within its confines and show no evidence of being crushed by it. Some rebellion comes, and should be expected, from teen-age boys.

Amish children are happy, they do not feel defrauded, they are not envious of other children who have "everything." They are surprisingly objective and unselfish about wanting things for themselves, because the first lesson they learn is self-denial. Work is an accepted part of their life. Even toddlers look forward impatiently to the time when they can take on the work of their elders. Besides obedience, the children early learn the real meaning of responsibility. They do not work because they must, but because it is a habit which they enjoy.

Instead of being "piously sober" or crushed and repressed, as one might expect in a strict religious sect, Amish children are gay, lively and full of fun. They laugh and giggle, they play jokes and tricks, they tease each other unmercifully (and often unkindly). They know how to make their own fun, they do not need to have it manufactured for them. Their play is vivacious and energetic—a favorite game of the girls is baseball.

I was astonished at the vigor of certain children. Most of them are thin and wiry—I was told it was because they work so hard and are always so active. (I saw some who showed evidence of undernourishment and lack of sufficient sleep and rest.) Light of movement, swift of foot, running like the wind, everything they did from batting a ball to pumping the old iron pump at school, from pitching hay in the barn (a five-year-old boy) to taking down an Amish bonnet from a shelf, was done with gusto and vigor. Many of the children are painfully shy and quiet, but those who have had contact with tourists and "strangers" are friendly and outgoing, without being bold. It was a joy to be with them and share their interests and activities. My one regret was that I could not understand their give-and-take speech with each other, because it was in Pennsylvania Dutch. In this I missed a good deal.

A widespread misconception confuses the term "Pennsylvania Dutch" with "Amish." These terms are not synonymous. "Pennsylvania Dutch" includes many sects. Only a very small portion of the Pennsylvania Dutch, or German, people can properly be called Amish.

The Pennsylvania Dutch speech is not Holland Dutch at all, nor is it German, but a mixture of German dialects with English and a special intonation of its own. It is a softer language than guttural High German. It is used in all Amish homes, but the children learn English quickly at school and speak it without accent. I did not hear any of the overpublicized "Pennsylvania Dutch dialect" expressions used by Amish

people in Lancaster County. Their English was singularly free of Ger-
man accent or construction or influence.

It should be understood that the customs and habits of the "Pennsyl-
vania Dutch" or the "gay Dutch" are quite different from those of the
Amish, or "the plain people." The "gay Dutch" speak with a pro-
nounced German accent, the Amish with little or none. The "gay
Dutch" are far more "worldly" than the Amish.

I was told that tourists in Lancaster County often incorrectly pro-
nounce the word Ā-mish, to the annoyance of the people. The word is
Ah-mish. Amish children call their parents by Pennsylvania Dutch
words: Dăt (rhymes with cat*) for* father, *and* Mam *(rhymes with* ham*)*
for mother. *These are used throughout my story.*

The Amish call all non-Amish people, or outsiders, "English." The
word does not mean British, *or "citizen of England." It simply means*
any person who is not Amish and speaks English. The word is used in
this sense in my book.

I have chosen Amish names for my characters at random. Since there
is so much duplication of both given names and surnames among the
Amish, it is possible that my names may coincide with those of living
people. This is unintentional, as they are all made-up names. All
my characters are fictional, and none are based on actual living people;
many are composites. Although my characters are fictional, the things
they do and the things that happen in my story are true, as they have all
happened to living persons in the region. Those who told me of these
happenings were willing to have them recounted in this book. The
title of my book was chosen by my Amish friends. I feel it is a singu-
larly happy and appropriate one.

There are many variations in Amish customs among Amish people
living in different areas of Pennsylvania and other states. My book is
an attempt to depict correctly the customs of the Amish in one district
of Lancaster County, Pennsylvania, only, with the help of the people
who live there.

All observations and conclusions regarding the Amish way of life stated here are my own and have not been taken from printed sources.

The making of a good shoo-fly pie is an art, but one easily acquired by quite young Amish girls. I hope that my women and girl readers will feel inspired to try this authentic recipe:

Shoo-Fly Pie

Mix 1 cup flour, 2/3 cup brown sugar, 1 tablespoon butter into crumbs. Set aside half the mixture. Mix 1 cup dark molasses, 3/4 cup boiling water, 1 teaspoon soda, 1 beaten egg. Then mix with half the crumbs, but do not beat. Put in pie shell and cover with the remaining crumbs. Bake 11 minutes at 375° and 30 minutes at 350°.

Lois Lenski

Lancaster County, Pennsylvania, September 1962
Tarpon Springs, Florida, Winter 1962–1963

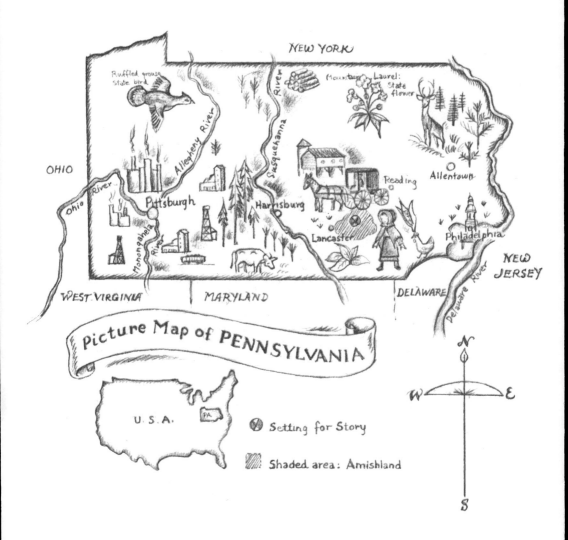

NEW YORK

Ruffled grouse
State bird

Mountain Laurel:
State
flower

Allegheny River

Susquehanna River

OHIO

Ohio River

Reading

Allentown

Pittsburgh

Harrisburg

Monongahela River

Lancaster

Philadelphia

WEST VIRGINIA

MARYLAND

DELAWARE

NEW JERSEY

Delaware River

Picture Map of PENNSYLVANIA

U.S.A.

PA.

N
W   E
S

⊗ Setting for Story

▨ Shaded area: Amishland

Shoo-Fly Girl

The world is too much with us; late and soon,
Getting and spending, we lay waste our powers:
Little we see in Nature that is ours;
We have given our hearts away, a sordid boon!
                              —William Wordsworth

Shall she not find in comforts of the sun,
In pungent fruit and bright, green wings, or else
In any balm or beauty of the earth,
Things to be cherished like the thought of Heaven?
                              —Wallace Stevens

The World Is Small and Safe

CHAPTER I

The Familiar Path

"*A ch*, don't pull so!" cried Suzanna.

"Stand still, once," said her older sister. "Stop wiggling."

The big kitchen was a busy place. The children were getting up. It was still dark outside, so the lamp over the table was lit.

Bib and Beck, the two big girls, whose real names were Barbara and Rebecca, were already dressed. Beck and the boys had gone outside with their father and mother to milk the cows. The twins sat half dressed on the floor playing. Henry, five, snatched his hat and ran out too. Sammy, three, still in bed, began to cry.

Bib dipped the comb into the basin. She parted Suzanna's hair and began to wet it. She made neat twists over each ear and pulled them back.

"Not so tight! Not so tight!" cried Suzanna.

Bib made two long braids in back, coiled them in a knot and pinned it with hairpins.

"There now, Susie," she said. "You're done."

"Why do you make it so fierce tight?" asked Suzanna. "I can't even turn my head! It hurts terrible!"

But Bib paid no attention. "Who's next? Punkin or Puddin?"

The twins, age seven, looked just alike. They had the same blue eyes, the same brown hair, the same pointed chins and fat cheeks. They were the same height too. Their real names, Anna and Ada, were seldom used. When they were fat babies, Uncle Dave had called them Punkin and Puddin, and the names had stuck. The Fishers loved nicknames.

Bib, who was fourteen, had plenty to do. She was frying mush for breakfast, trying to comb the twins' hair and pack the school lunches all at once.

"Put in a piece of shoo-fly pie for me," said Suzanna.

"*Ach* now, all you want is shoo-fly pie," said Bib. "We've only got one and it's not enough for breakfast. Here, put it on the table. I'll bake some more today after school and you can help me."

She handed a large pie with a crumby top to her sister.

"Punkin and Puddin, get the table set," called Bib. "Hurry a little or we'll all be late for school."

The little girls took knives, forks and plates to the long table by the window. They hopped up and down on the long benches. They were very light on their bare feet. They set eleven places— there were nine children and Dat and Mam.

It was getting light now and the others came in. Mam put out the light in the gas lamp as the morning sun streamed in through the east window. Then she brought Sammy from his bed. Everybody washed at the basin and sat down.

All but Suzanna. She was not there. They never started a meal until all were there.

"Where's that girl?" asked Mam. "Beck, Bib, where is she?"

"*Susie! Susie!*" Bib called.

The door of the kettle house opened and Suzanna came running. She slid into place on the girls' bench.

"Move over!" she said, licking her lips. "Gimme room, Punkin."

"Silence!" said Dat. "Hands on laps. Fold your hands."

They bowed their heads. Mam and Dat moved their lips and prayed silently, eyes closed. The children prayed too, without a sound. Then they reached for food and ate. They spread pork pudding on fried mush and ate it. They had "coffee soup"— coffee poured over bread cubes. All but Suzanna, who licked her lips again. She was not hungry. She hoped no one would notice.

"Clean your plates," said Dat.

Nobody talked. They were too hungry, too busy eating.

Suzanna slid her slice of mush onto Reuben's plate. He wolfed it down. Nobody saw.

"Heck! No pie this morning?" cried Jonas.

Jonas was the oldest, fifteen. He liked to think himself a man, just because he was through school. He had finished the eighth grade and did not have to go any more.

"Who's hiding the shoo-fly pie this morning?" asked Dat. Breakfast was not breakfast without it.

"Why, Suzanna!" said Bib. "I gave it to you to put on the table." She looked but there was no pie in sight. "What did you do with it?"

Suzanna jumped up, ready to be off. Then she knew there was no escape. She must stay at table until everyone had finished eating and they had prayed again. She sat down.

Mam repeated the question. "What did you do with the pie, Susie?"

Suzanna hesitated. Then she wailed, "Do we have to have pie *every* day for breakfast?"

"That's not the point," said Mam. *"What did you do with it?"*

Suzanna hung her head. They were all looking at her now. "I hid it."

"Hid it? Where?" asked Mam.

"In the kettle house," said Suzanna.

"Go get it then," said Mam. "Why on earth did you hide it?"

Oh dear, Mam always had to know everything. "Because . . . because . . . I dropped it!" said Suzanna.

She might as well tell it all. There could never be any secrets in *this* house. "I *dropped* it and *smashed* it . . . and then . . . and then . . ." She might as well confess. "It wasn't any good for anything . . . so I picked it up . . . and . . ."

"Then what?" asked Dat. He spoke in a gentle voice, not scolding at all.

"Then I just ate it up!"

The words sounded frightening in the silence. Suzanna looked at Mam, lips set tight and black frown getting blacker. She was in for it now. She'd get a terrible licking. Eating a whole pie! Who ever heard of such a thing?

But thunder and lightning did not strike.

Out of the silence came a cackle of laughter.

It was Rags, Reuben by **name**, whose laugh was like a hen

cackling. Then Dat began to roar and all the others joined in. Suzanna looked up and saw a broad smile on her mother's face. She was safe—no yardstick this time!

"So that's why you weren't hungry for breakfast!" said Mam. "You were full of shoo-fly pie!"

They laughed and laughed. Would they never get done laughing? What was so funny about eating pie? No licking, thought Suzanna, but this might be worse. They would tease her to death.

"Hi, Shoo-Fly!" cried Jonas, the biggest tease of all. "Been shooin' any flies lately?"

"She's got her tummy full of shoo-fly," cried Rags.

They pointed their fingers and Susie wept.

She had earned a permanent nickname. From this time on her name was seldom Suzanna or even Susie. It was Shoo-Fly.

Bib did not forget. Bib never forgot anything. That day after school, she saw to it that Suzanna made a shoo-fly pie, her first. It was Friday, baking day. Mam had been baking bread all day long in the big oven in the kettle house. Bib had to bake the cakes and pies. They were getting ready for Saturday. They would sell them at the pie stand on the highway.

Suzanna Fisher, formerly called Susie and now Shoo-Fly, was a little Amish girl. She lived on a farm in Lancaster County, Pennsylvania. Her parents, grandparents and all her ancestors had been Amish since they came to America from Switzerland in the early 1700s. They were a strict religious sect who lived as close to the teachings of the Bible as they knew how. They kept themselves apart from the world and its ways. They had a way of life all their own. The Amish children were used to hard work. As soon as they could walk, they had chores of their own to do.

Suzanna had made *schnitz* or dried apple pies before. They were easy. A shoo-fly pie was different and took longer. Bib told her just how to do it. How to mix brown sugar, flour and butter to make the crumbs. How to mix molasses with hot water and soda and pour it in a pastry shell. Then put the crumby mixture on top and bake it.

"Why do they call it *shoo-fly* pie?" asked Suzanna.

Bib shook her head. "Don't ask me!" she said. Bib was always serious. "That's its name. We've always called it that."

It was the same answer Suzanna always got. Why do we wear black bonnets? We've always done so. Why do we wear black aprons? We've always done so. Why do we have church in a house and not in a church? Why do we do things this way? We've always done it this way. Our grandparents and great-grandparents did it this way. So we do it too. We are Amish. We do not change. Suzanna had heard it over and over. She would hear it all her life. She would say it to her children.

"But *why* do they call it shoo-fly pie?" she asked again. "*I* know. Because it's so good, the flies like it—and you have to shoo them away."

Bib looked at her smiling.

"You ought to know how good it is," she said. "You ate a whole pie."

On Saturday, Bib had to stay home and do the Saturday cleaning. Besides, Bib liked housework and Beck didn't. So Beck hitched the horse Skipper to the carriage and packed the bread, cakes and pies in the back. Mam told Suzanna she could go along. But she did not want to go.

"I want to stay here," she said. "I want to see Grossmama and Aunt Suzanna . . . I want to help them . . . They need me. . . ."

She tried to think up excuses, but the truth was she did not like to go away at all. Out on the highway where all the cars were, she was frightened. She was scared of strangers too. No telling what they might do or say. It was bad enough to have to go to school. Home was the best place, the safest place to be.

But Suzanna had to obey. Like every Amish child, she had to obey without question. She put on her long purple school dress and black apron, she tied her purple bonnet under her chin. She heard her mother talking to Rebecca. Talking about *her*.

"It will soon be Suzanna's turn. She is old enough, she can make change. She can do the selling from now on, once she learns how."

Make change! Do the selling! Talk to strangers? Was Mam crazy? What was she thinking of?

"Get a move on, Shoo-Fly. Mam's waiting!" called Rags outside holding the horse.

Suzanna climbed into the buggy. She sat down in the back next to the boxes of baked goods. She was hemmed in by the darkness. She could not see a thing. The buggy had covered top and sides, and the curtain was down at the back. It was like a little house. There was one little window to peek out of. It was a good place to hide. It would be a good place to lie down and sleep—if they'd only let her.

Skipper's hoofs made a steady *clop-clopping* down the lane and out on the road. The buggy wheels squeaked and crunched on the loose gravel. Mam and Beck talked in low voices. After a while they made a turn and started again on the paved road. Soon a loud roar like that of a lion was heard, and a big automobile came bearing down on them. Suzanna could hear it, even if she could not see it. It was a big monster going to eat them. . . . She held her breath. But it went on by and left her to her dreams. Other cars came and went but she did not notice them.

All too soon they came to a stop. Everybody piled out at the pie stand. It was like a little table with a roof on top. Dat and

Uncle Chris had made it. Beck unhitched Skipper and backed the buggy up behind. She and Mam took the baked goods and vegetables out. Also jars of Mam's apple and pear butter, cherry and plum jam. They set them on the stand. Beck fixed them to look nice. She and Mam talked about prices.

Cars began to stop. The people in them were not Amish. They did not speak Dutch, so the Amish people called them "English"—because they all spoke English. Suzanna spoke English too—at school. She could read and write and spell it. But at home she spoke in Dutch. These people who spoke English all the time were queer. They wore fancy clothes in gay patterns and bright colors. When Suzanna asked about it, her mother said, "They are not like us. We are the plain people. We are Amish." The same answer over and over again.

Each time a car stopped, Suzanna hid. Sometimes she climbed in "her house" in the buggy. Sometimes she had only time to duck under the counter, so people would not see her. Mam had to explain, "She's terrible bashful—this one."

When they were alone, Mam told her, "You must learn how to sell the pie and cake."

"*Ach,* no!" The thought terrified her. "I can't!"

Mam told her the prices. "Cake $1.25, corn 50¢ a dozen, bread 25¢, pie 85¢." Suzanna repeated the prices after her. She looked at Beck's black pocketbook on a long shoulder strap. It might be fun to wear it. It might be fun, after all, to jingle the coins and make change. . . .

"Stand here," said Mam. "Don't you go hide. You might as

well get used to strangers. They won't bite you. Stand here and shoo the flies away." She gave her a piece of paper.

Just then a man came up. He got out of the largest black car Suzanna had ever seen. The man had no beard and wore no hat. How funny he looked! He was fat and had a gold pin in his bright red tie. He had a big cigar in his mouth and kept puffing. Mam was fixing things in the buggy. She turned her back to him.

For an Amish girl, Beck was very bold. Mam had told her how to talk to tourists. "Where are you from, Mister?" she asked.

"Massachusetts," the man said.

"You're a long ways from home," said Beck. That was what you said to all of them.

The man looked at Beck. He saw her bonnet and cape and apron.

"You're Amish," he said. "What's your name?"

"Rebecca Fisher," said Beck in a low voice. "What's yours?"

"I'm not telling," said the man.

Then he saw Suzanna shooing the flies away.

"What's *your* name?" he asked.

Suzanna ducked behind Beck and did not answer.

"Cat's got your tongue!" teased the man.

Suzanna peeked around and stuck out her tongue at him. There! That would stop him. Why should he know her name? He was a stranger.

"*Ach,* Susie!" scolded Beck under her breath. "Don't act so. He won't buy anything!"

"You don't need to tell me your name," said the man. "I know it already. You're *Shoo-Fly Girl,* because you shoo the flies away."

How did *he* know? Could he read people's minds? Did he know she ate a whole shoo-fly pie just yesterday? How did he ever guess her nickname?

"Shoo-Fly Girl!" said the man again.

Beck laughed. Mam heard and laughed too. Suzanna hated him. She'd never be Suzanna or Susie any more. She'd always be Shoo-Fly.

"Shoo-Fly made the shoo-fly pie!" Beck lifted it up. "That's for sure!"

"She did?" he said. "That little thing? No bigger than a minute? Can she bake pies? I'll take it."

He paid the money, took the pie and went back to his car.

After they were sold out, Mam and Beck and Shoo-Fly drove home again. Everything looked just the same, the big "bank" barn, the windmill, the double house, the four big martin boxes on tall poles in the barnyard. Why couldn't the martins stay longer? Suzanna liked to watch them swoop across the sky and come back down to their houses. She looked at her own house— the house so plain, no curtains, with green shades pulled down halfway, neat and clean, the house called home.

It was noon and Bib had dinner ready. After dinner, Shoo-Fly skipped out. Saturday, no school, a time to be free and do as you please. Mam had sewing to do—that would keep her indoors. The sewing for nine children, making all their clothes, was never done. Bib and Beck put on their oldest clothes and went out to the tobacco field.

"I don't want to work, do you?" said Shoo-Fly to Rags.

"No," said Rags, "but we'll have to."

He had his raggediest clothes on, ready for whatever might come. He did not have as many ideas for escaping work as Shoo-Fly did.

"I'll tell you what," said Shoo-Fly. "We'll rub our arms with poison ivy, then we won't have to help."

"O.K.," said Rags. He cackled with glee. "Where will we find some?"

Shoo-Fly led the way to a shady place down by the creek. She picked bunches of three-pointed leaves, crushed them between stones and rubbed the paste on Rags's arms and her own. It colored them nice and green. She rubbed it on their bare legs and feet too.

"Now we're safe," she said.

"But won't it hurt?" asked Rags. "I had it once and it itched me terrible."

"It goes away soon," said Shoo-Fly. "Now we can go out and watch the others work."

Shoo-Fly liked to be out where the others were. She did not want to miss anything. It was a wonderful September day, crisp and cool, but sunny. She went tearing across to the tobacco field. She was so thin and her feet were so light, they hardly touched the ground. Rags came too, but more slowly. He liked to take his time. Then came Henry and Sammy and behind them, Pretzel, barking loudly. Pretzel, a nondescript dog, got his name because he liked to eat pretzels.

Henry, only five, was not called Hayfork for nothing. He could handle a man's hayfork like a man. His blond bobbed hair made a halo around his smiling face under the broad brim of his black felt hat. He always wore his hat outdoors.

The children ran to the field and stopped.

The tobacco had been cut and the men were working at the far end of the five-acre field. Dat was not a farmer like Uncle Chris. He had a carriage shop and Uncle Chris farmed the farm. But today Dat was out helping. Beck and Bib were helping too. The tobacco had to be cut and hung up in the shed and barn to dry before frost.

Everybody was working fast. The stalks that stood so strong
and tall now lay on the ground. The workers speared them, five
stalks to a lath. The girls wore old gray aprons up to their necks.
They had red kerchiefs tied over their hair.

"We'd better not go too close," said Rags.

"Hi, you kids, come over here and get to work!" called Bib.

"I told you so," said Rags.

Bib called again. They went up closer, but not too close.

"We can't work," said Shoo-Fly. "We've got poison ivy. Our
arms and legs are sore. They itch terrible!" She showed Bib her
arms, but Bib just laughed.

"Another one of your tricks," she said, but she let them alone.

"Let's go play on the wagon," said Hayfork.

They climbed on the tobacco wagon and helped little Sammy

up. They jumped down from the wagon and climbed up again.
They jumped up and down. It was fun. Pretzel barked madly.

Then Beck called. "Come here, Shoo-Fly, and get to work.
We are loading now and you can help."

Dat came up and said, "Come, girl, we need all the help we
can get."

"I told you so," said Rags.

Poison ivy or no poison ivy, Shoo-Fly had to obey. She picked
up a lath and speared five tobacco plants on it. The loaded lath
was heavy, but she lifted it up to the wagon. Hayfork helped
her. "I'm as strong as a man!" he bragged.

Then he and Shoo-Fly began to load the girls' laths on the
wagon. It made good teamwork. But they soon grew tired.
Shoo-Fly whispered in Hayfork's ear. They had worked long
enough. His smile beamed approval. The next minute they
both jumped down from the wagon and went running across the
field. Sammy tagged behind. Rags kept right on working.

"Let's go to the carriage shop," said Shoo-Fly.

Hayfork nodded. "And see Jonas," he said.

Uncle Chris was Dat's brother. He and Aunt Emma lived out
by the road, near the carriage shop. Their children were still
babies. Dat made and repaired Amish carriages and buggies.
Jonas helped in the shop or on the farm wherever needed. The
shop was always full of all kinds of buggies, old, new, broken
down or half finished. It was a good place to play.

Jonas was there today mixing paint. Dat's helper, old Ephraim
Esh, was inside working at the forge.

"*Ach,* see Cousin Eli's pony cart!" cried Shoo-Fly.

Hayfork and Shoo-Fly stared. The new cart stood outside in the sun. It was beautiful—shiny black with red trim. It had lamps on the sides, electric, fed from batteries under the seat. Jonas came out and showed them everything.

"It's just finished," he said. "Watch out for wet paint!"

"*Ach,* Jonas!" cried Shoo-Fly. "Such a cart for . . ."

"Too good for that little spoiled brat, Eli," said Jonas.

"Eli gets what he wants," said Hayfork. At five, Henry was wise beyond his years.

Eli was their cousin, Uncle Dave's older son. Eli had a brown and white pony called Buster. Now Eli was getting a new pony cart. Uncle Dave had ordered it from Dat.

"Give us a ride in it, Jonas!" begged Hayfork, starting to pick up the shafts. "Be a pony and pull us."

"Drop it!" cried Jonas. "The paint's not dry."

Hayfork jumped back.

Across the road from Uncle Chris's house and the shop stood another farmhouse. A large truck pulled out of its lane and went rattling down the road. The house had been empty for some time.

"New people just moved in," said Jonas, looking up.

"Somebody we know?" asked Shoo-Fly.

"No," said Jonas. "They're 'English.' "

"Oh!" said Shoo-Fly, disappointed. She saw the door open and several children come out. "There's a girl," she said.

"There's a boy about my age and some little ones," said Jonas.

"Where they from?" asked Shoo-Fly.

"I don't know," said Jonas.

The new children were curious. They came out their lane and walked along the road. They came closer and closer to the carriage shop, as if half afraid. They came as close as they dared. They did not speak.

Shoo-Fly and her brothers watched them come. The girl was about Shoo-Fly's age, ten or so, the others younger. They looked at the pony cart. They looked at Shoo-Fly and her brothers. Jonas and Hayfork and Shoo-Fly began to talk in Pennsylvania Dutch.

Then the girl spoke. "What's that lingo you're speaking? What are you talking about?" She could not understand Dutch.

No one answered. She turned to her little sister and said,

"Listen to their funny talk!"

Her little brother had darted into the shop.

"Where's my brother?" the girl called. "Where's Robert?"

Shoo-Fly flew with her into the shop.

There was Robert with little Sammy. They had found an open can of black grease. They had smeared it all over their faces and clothes. They were black and sticky from head to foot.

"Oh! Oh!" cried the girl. "Look at Robert!"

Shoo-Fly knew just what to do. She found some lava soap that Dat and Jonas used. She washed the grease off the boys' hands and faces. But she could not get it off their clothes.

The strange girl took her brother and sister and went home. She did not say anything.

"They're mad at us," said Shoo-Fly.

"Who cares?" laughed Jonas.

It was on the way home that Jonas found the crow. A flock of crows was circling around a tree, cawing loudly. Then they took wing and darted low across the field. The boys began throwing stones at them. Suddenly one dropped to the ground.

"*Ach*, you killed it!" cried Shoo-Fly.

Hayfork picked the crow up and gave it to Jonas.

"Is it dead, Jonas?" asked Shoo-Fly.

"No," said Jonas, "only stunned. It's not hurt at all. There's not a drop of blood."

"There! It's opening its eyes," said Shoo-Fly. "It's alive."

"It's a young crow, about half grown," said Jonas.

"Give it to me," said the girl.

Jonas and Hayfork went running ahead across the field. Shoo-
Fly cuddled the crow in her apron.

"I'll tame it," she said. "I'll have a pet all my own."

She walked slowly and the world was filled with the song of
birds, the smell of the good earth and the warm glow of the
setting sun.

CHAPTER II

A Step to One Side

N obody liked the crow but Shoo-Fly. The more the others
hated it, the more she loved it.

That first day she fed it bread and milk. She spooned food
and water into its bill. She made a straw bed in a little chicken
pen for it. The front was made of wire, so the bird could not
get out. Each day the crow grew stronger. Soon it began to
know her and to make noises.

When she let it out, the little boys and the twins teased it and chased it. Punkin pulled a feather out and the crow pecked her. Puddin squeezed it hard and it bit her. So they soon learned to let it alone.

Shoo-Fly took it out each day and put it back in its pen at night. It was a great comfort to her. It was wonderful to have something that nobody else wanted. This was an important thing to learn in a large family.

Now Jonas had something new to tease her about. Whenever he saw the crow, he shouted, "Hi, Shoo-Fly! Come shoo this old black thief away!"

Shoo-Fly teased Jonas too. "What's that black fuzz on your chin, Jonas? Are you growing a beard, so you can go courting?"

But Jonas always had an answer. "When I grow up," he said, "I'm going to wear neckties and buttons, cut my hair short and shave off my beard!"

It was a daring threat and Shoo-Fly was shocked. Amish men did not wear neckties and had hooks and eyes on their outer clothes in place of buttons. They all had beards and wore their hair loose and full.

"You gonna be 'English'?" cried Shoo-Fly.

Jonas only laughed.

The next day Shoo-Fly saw the new children again—at school. Just before the last bell rang, their mother drove up in a big green car and they jumped out. Their mother talked to Miss Weber, then drove away.

Shoo-Fly and Reuben and the twins went to Meadowbrook School. It had one room and six grades. Most of the children were Amish, but not all. Beck and Bib went to a small junior high for Amish children. Shoo-Fly liked her teacher even if she wasn't Amish. Miss Weber's hair hung in soft waves to her shoulders. Her cheeks were pink and she wore pretty silk dresses.

At school, Shoo-Fly was still Suzanna. Miss Weber did not like nicknames.

When school took up, all the children came running in pell-mell, and took their seats. There in the empty seat beside Suzanna sat the new girl. Betty Ferguson, Miss Weber said her name was. She was in the fourth grade too. Suzanna paid no attention to her.

Until recess, when Betty smiled and put her arm around Suzanna.

"I didn't know you could speak English," said Betty.

"Why, sure," said Suzanna. "Why not?"

"You'll be my girlfriend, won't you?" asked Betty.

The others were calling. Suzanna ran to the cupboard and got ball and bat and baseball gloves. She ran out and started a ball game in the high grass. All the Amish girls were good ball players. The new children stood and watched.

Suzanna loved to play ball. She bossed the other children around, even the "English" boys. In the middle of the game, a gray car drove up and stopped. The children looked, then went on with their game. A man got out with a large black box and started fussing.

"It's a camera!" Amos Zook said, just loud enough for all to hear. Amos was the son of the Amish Bishop in this district, so

the children listened. The game broke up. The children huddled together, heads turned, a whisper or two, then they scattered
like dry leaves in a gusty wind. One minute they were there, and
the next minute when the man had his camera all set and looked
up, they were gone. There was nothing to take a picture of.

Suzanna ran the fastest. She took the twins by the hand and
dragged them inside the school. Miss Weber came to see.

Shoo-Fly said, "Photographs are wicked. We all ran. 'He
was a tourist!"

Miss Weber smiled. She understood.

"But what did they run for?"

There was that new girl again, wanting to know everything.

"Photographs are wicked," said Shoo-Fly. "It says so in the
Bible!"

"Oh!" said Betty. "Does it?"

After the man left, the boys began playing *horse.* With binders' twine for harness, they drove each other madly about, stamping and prancing. Then the bell rang and it was time to go in. The children lined up at the iron pump to wash. Amos Zook, John Esh and Reuben pumped. The children washed their hands and drank from cupped fingers. They ran indoors, panting.

That day was a happy one for Suzanna, because Miss Weber gave her a new storybook to take home. She looked at the title, *Rebecca of Sunnybrook Farm!* Rebecca! It must be about an Amish girl! There were many Amish Rebeccas. She patted the book lovingly.

The new girl looked at it too.

"That book's no good," she said. "It's stupid! Why don't you get a *mystery* book? Or a *horse* book? I like *horse* books, I just love horses!"

It was time to go. Three little Amish girls took brooms, dustpans and dustcloths to clean the schoolroom. Suzanna stepped on a chair at the back of the room. She got the twins' bonnets down from the shelf, and her own. She looked at the initials inside to get the right ones. She got Reuben's hat down too.

The boys ran for their homemade scooters. Quickly Reuben took off shoes and stockings and hung them across the scooter handle. He set his lunchbox at the base, and with the other boys, went dashing off, coattails flying and black felt hats tipped on backs of their heads. The girls were soon left far behind.

"Go ahead!" Suzanna told her little sisters. "Go ahead with the other girls. I'm not in a hurry today."

They started down the road, a colorful group of bonneted and aproned little girls wearing dark bonnets, sweaters and shawls. A few had black shoes and stockings, but most were barefoot. Suzanna brought up the rear.

"I hope that new girl won't come and talk to me," she said to herself. Looking back, she saw Betty Ferguson still in the schoolroom, talking to Miss Weber. "Teacher's pet!" she said aloud.

Shoo-Fly walked slowly, reading her book. It was not about an Amish girl, after all. But oh, it was good, good, good! How would she ever find time to read it? Once home, there were all those chores waiting, nothing but work, work, work, no time to read at all. Mam and Dat thought books were a waste of time. So her nose dipped lower and lower and her steps grew slower and slower. Better read while she had the chance.

Suddenly she bumped into something. She looked up and found herself in the ditch, with her nose against a tree! Oh dear, did anybody see her? They would say she was *ferhoodlt!* Back in the road, a sharp honk made her jump to one side. It was that new girl's mother, heading for the school.

She saw the Amish girls ahead huddled in a group. She closed her book and ran ahead to join them. They had stopped at a telephone pole. This was something new to them, as none of the Amish farms had telephones. A new line had just been put in to the Fergusons' house. Shoo-Fly knew all about it. A telephone was something you talked into. You talked to people far away. The talk went over the telephone wires. If you put your ear up close to the pole, you could hear what the people were

saying. The Amish girls listened one by one, but they all shook
their heads.

"We can't make out what they're sayin'."

"Here! Let me once!" Shoo-Fly did everything with vigor.
She pushed the other girls away, shoved her bonnet back and put
her ear close to the pole.

"They're talking in Greek," she announced, her eyes open wide.
"No, it's French, I think. Wait a minute, it sounds like Italian!
They say there's a bad snowstorm over there and everybody is
snowed under and an avalanche is sliding down the mountain
and going to bury a whole town full of people . . ."

Her eyes gleamed as the story got bigger and bigger.

"I don't believe a word of it!" snapped Katie Zook. "You're
makin' all that up."

"Yes, well," Shoo-Fly went on, "it could be any language at all. . . . Miss Weber said we've got Greeks and French and Italians and Polish and all kinds of people in our country, the whole world is not all just Pennsylvania Dutch like you, Katie Zook. . . ."

But Katie was far on down the road, not listening at all.

Just then a car came speeding up. It was the big green one again. Mrs. Ferguson had picked up Betty and her little brother and sister at school and was taking them home. The car stopped beside the group of girls.

"Suzanna, would you like a ride home?" asked Mrs. Ferguson. She opened the car door and Betty begged her to get in.

The temptation was too great to be resisted. Katie Zook was not asked to ride, only Suzanna Fisher. *I'll show her!* thought

Shoo-Fly. The next minute she was in the car, sitting on the shiny soft green cushion beside Betty. Before Mrs. Ferguson started on, Shoo-Fly heard the twins crying and the taunts of the other girls.

"Suzanna wants to be 'English'!"

"I'll tell your Mam! You'll get a licking!"

But she held up her head in pride. She was the *only* one asked to ride.

It was Shoo-Fly's first ride in an automobile. The car slid along so nice and smooth and even. There were no bumps at all. Everything went by so fast—the trees, the fences, the corn in the fields, a house or two—she could hardly see them. Betty kept on talking, but she did not hear. Then all at once she was frightened. The car went fast and kept on going faster. Mrs. Ferguson wasn't looking at the road. She kept turning around and talking to the girls in the back seat.

And there ahead, out from a side lane came an Amish buggy. The car almost hit it! Shoo-Fly trembled in fright. Why, it was her own lane and that was Grossmama in her buggy driving her horse Sonny Boy. Shoo-Fly gasped! Her face went white. The car came near to hitting Grossmama!

The danger was over now. The car had passed the buggy safely. Shoo-Fly had waved weakly, but Grossmama did not see her. Grossmama did not look at people riding in cars.

Then Mrs. Ferguson slowed down. "I went past your lane," she said. "I'll have to turn around. We'll go in. I want to meet your mother."

Shoo-Fly could not answer. She could not seem to find words.

Mam was in the house yard taking down the clothes. She had washed that morning. She had to wash three times a week. Somebody had let the geese out. There were thirty of them. They were supposed to stay in their own fenced field. Now they were all over the yard, cackling and making a mess on the cement sidewalk. Mam was waiting for the children to come home to pen them up again.

The place looked terrible.

Mrs. Ferguson stopped in the barnyard beside the row of martin box poles. Mam came out to meet the car. She had her white prayer covering on, tied in a bow hanging below her chin. But her dress and apron were not clean. She probably thought it was an egg customer. What she saw surprised her.

"You must be Mrs. Fisher," said Mrs. Ferguson, brightly. "I'm your new neighbor, Dolly Ferguson."

Politely, Mam shook her hand. "Pleased to meet you, Mrs. Ferguson."

The air was filled with ice.

"I brought your little girl home from school," said Mrs. Ferguson, "in my car."

"I see you did." Mam's mouth was a thin line. Her face froze. Shoo-Fly climbed out. Mam looked down at her daughter. "Suzanna rode home in your *car?*"

"Yes, she hitchhiked with me!" said Mrs. Ferguson with a laugh. "Is that something terrible?"

Mam looked at Suzanna again.

"I thought she knew better," she said slowly. Then to Mrs. Ferguson, "She's young yet, but she'll learn."

"Learn what?" asked Mrs. Ferguson, baffled.

"Not to ride in cars," said Mam, quietly and with pride. "It is not our way. We do not ride in cars. We are Amish."

"Oh! I'm sorry," said Mrs. Ferguson. "Is it wicked?"

"It is not necessary," said Mam. "We ride in cars only in case of emergency. Please do not pick her up again. Suzanna has two good legs. She can walk."

Coldly Mrs. Ferguson turned away. How could she ever be friends with these queer people? When you try to do them a kindness . . .

Shoo-Fly walked in the house slowly, hugging her new book in her arms. Reuben and the twins came home, then the older girls. They all made a dash for the big pretzel can in the kitchen. They filled their mouths with salty pretzels and all talked at once —in English.

Mam came in frowning. She heard their English talk.

"We are Dutch," she said. "We don't speak English here."

The talk simmered down into the soft tones of Pennsylvania Dutch.

Shoo-Fly grabbed a handful of pretzels and stuffed them into the secret pocket under her apron. She took another handful and stuffed them into her mouth. Mam looked so cross, Shoo-Fly was afraid to say a word. She slipped out the side door when no one was looking.

She would go and see Grossmama. Grossmama was a good friend in time of need.

Grossmama and Aunt Suzanna lived in the Grossdawdy house. The Fishers' house was a double one, two houses joined together. Grossdawdy, who was dead now, had built his house first. Then when he got too old to farm, he joined another house on, for his youngest son, Rufus. That was Shoo-Fly's father, whom the children called Dat. Aunt Suzanna was Dat's sister, and little Suzanna, or Shoo-Fly, had been named for her. Aunt Suzanna and Grossmama lived together now in the Grossdawdy house.

Shoo-Fly ran around the corner and in at the door, but the big kitchen was empty. Where was Grossmama?

There was her rocking chair beside the window, with the ferns and potted plants. There was her sewing basket, her thimble and scissors. The fire was burning in the range and something was cooking in the big pot. The kettle was singing comfortably. The room was quiet, peaceful, still. Only the big clock on the high shelf made a noise, ticking steadily. Then it growled and struck the hour, a lonely sound.

Shoo-Fly's heart sank and tears came to her eyes. Where was Grossmama? She wanted to be a little girl again, to sit on Grossmama's lap and feel her warm arms around her. She wanted to talk things over.

But the house was empty. She called up the stairway. No one answered. Grossmama was gone.

Then Shoo-Fly remembered. She had seen Sonny Boy and the buggy go out the lane as she drove in with Mrs. Ferguson. Grossmama went riding in her buggy whenever she wanted to. She never told where she was going. Maybe she went to see Great-Grossmama or Uncle John, or the doctor or to the store. Maybe she just went to pick up Aunt Suzanna at the gift shop where she worked.

Grossmama would soon be back. She *had* to get back before sundown. She had no lamps on her buggy. She always stayed home after dark. So Shoo-Fly waited. She sat on the couch and waited in the gathering darkness. She ate her pretzels one by one. Then at last Grossmama came.

In she came, little, sprightly, brisk Grossmama, as chipper as a grasshopper. She took off her bonnet and shawl and hung them up. Then in came the twins, Punkin and Puddin, prancing and capering. The twins squealing and giggling. The twins chattering their heads off! Aunt Suzanna came in too.

Nobody noticed Shoo-Fly curled up on the couch. Or if they saw her, they ignored her. Grossmama started supper, while Aunt Suzanna pumped up the gas lamp and lighted it. Then she hung it over the table.

The twins were going to stay for supper. The twins had

brought their nightgowns with them . . . they were going to stay
all night . . . at Grossmama's. . . . The twins were spoiled rotten,
Mam always said.

Grossmama put wood on the fire, stirred the pot with a big
spoon, then sat down in her rocker and took the twins on her lap.
Big seven-year-old girls, two of them on her lap at once! She
rocked them back and forth. She began to sing to them:

> *Aw, ba, za,*
> *De kots lawft im shna,*
> *D'r shna gat avech,*
> *De kots lawft in dreck . . .*

A, B, C,
The cat walks in the snow,
The snow goes away
And the cat walks in the mud,
Jumps over the stump
with a bag full of rags,
Jumps over the barn
with a bag full of fire!

It was too much. Shoo-Fly couldn't stand it. She got up and started for the door.

"Where are you going, Susie?" called Grossmama, looking up. But it was too late now.

Shoo-Fly did not answer.

She went out and banged the door behind her.

Shoo-Fly did not get the threatened licking, nor did she ride in the Fergusons' car again. The next day at school, her life was miserable. The children teased her and never let up.

"Suzanna's trying to be English!" they cried.

She met every taunt with, *"Ach,* be still!" but that did not help much. Her only comfort was in her library book. That day she almost *ran* home from school. She couldn't wait to read more about Rebecca.

At home, the first thing she saw was that the yard was spotless. The geese were all in the goose run, and the walks had been scrubbed clean. There were three Amish buggies in the barn-yard. That meant company.

Before she went in, she took her crow out of his pen and turned him loose. He flew to a treetop and when she called him, he flew down and landed on her shoulder. He sat on her finger and ate corn out of her hand. But he would not let the twins hold him at all. He pecked at them instead. Before she put him back in his pen, she decided to name him Jackie.

She went in the kettle house, opened the kitchen door and took a peek. It was a quilting. Mam had her newest quilt on the frame in the front room. All seven aunts must be in there quilting. They were all talking at once. It sounded like birds making noises in a tree. The kitchen was big, as big as two average kitchens. It never looked bigger than now. It was filled with children. All the aunts had children, mostly babies . . . cousins . . . To Shoo-Fly babies meant bottles to be filled and diapers to be changed. She knew all about that! They were all crying and whining and fussing. She stepped over their heads, slid past the door opening into the front room and headed for the stairs.

There was only one thing to do—disappear. Hide where nobody would find her. How wonderful to have the library book! It was a good chance to read. The aunts must have been there for dinner. She glanced at the sink in passing. Why stay around when all those stacks and mounds of dishes were waiting? They hadn't even washed their own dishes or swept the floor after eating! Could it be they expected certain girls to come home from school and do it? Let them do it themselves! And if they stayed for supper, let them carry in their own wood, cook their food and wash dishes again!

Shoo-Fly crept quietly up the stairs.

She found her book and began to read. She changed to her old clothes as slowly as she could, reading as fast as she could. She was living with a non-Amish Rebecca on a non-Amish farm . . . oh, it was wonderful! This book-Rebecca rode on a stage, not in a buggy. . . .

Suddenly a voice broke into her dream.

"Suz-an-na! Suz-an-na!" It was Mam's voice calling. *"Suz-anna! Run down cellar and bring me a big jar of chow-chow!"*

Shoo-Fly had to think quickly. They'd find her up here in the bedroom, that's for sure. Beck and Bib would soon be home and come up here to change clothes. *They* could help Mam. It was time to disappear. But how? Where? Shoo-Fly had a number of favorite hiding places, but how to get to them?

Then an idea hit her. Clutching her book under her arm, she crept into the boys' bedroom. It was dark and spooky. Mam always kept the shades pulled. She stumbled and fell over big boys' shoes left in the middle of the floor, then got up. She saw a flashlight on Jonas' washstand and decided to borrow it. The window over the one-story kettle house could be opened. She could jump down on the lower roof and then from there to the ground. No sooner said than done.

Lucky she was a good jumper. She had had plenty of practice in the barn, taking dares from Jonas and Reuben. But in the barn there was hay to land on. Not hard ground barely covered with grass. The geese had nibbled it bare. She came down with a thump and frightened the geese. They all began to gobble. *Be quiet, you noisy things!* Her book fell, then the flashlight. *Ach! did I break it?* She picked them up and ran. She must get out of the goose run before anybody saw her. Pretzel chased her and began to bark.

Where to go? Which hidey-hole would be best?

Being the middle child in a family of nine, Shoo-Fly had problems. Her two big sisters and two big brothers thought she was too little to do what they did. Her two little sisters and two little brothers thought she was too big. She often found it hard to survive in a world all her own—smack in the middle.

The hidey-holes were a big help.

Which should it be? Where should she go? She had to think fast, before she got caught. Over to Grossmama's? No, not after last night. Behind the egg crates in the chicken house? No, it was too lousy there. Up in the haymow? The barn was full of tobacco now and smelled awful. Up in the cherry tree? They might see her there. How about the family buggy? Not Grossmama's but Mam's. It was in the barn. Mam would not be going anywhere as long as the aunts were there. No sooner said than done.

Shoo-Fly slipped in the side door of the barn and climbed into the buggy. Lucky she brought the flashlight along. It wasn't broken at all. Then she heard a noise, a squeaky noise, a whiny noise. Was it a cat mewing? She flashed her light on the buggy floor.

"Jeepers! Look there!" she cried. "It's Becky Green-Eyes and she's got kittens!"

There in a nice soft nest on the old horse blanket was Beck's cat that Jonas had named, with five baby kittens! They were squirming and mewing. Their eyes weren't open yet. She'd tell

Beck so she could feed them—but not now. Later on. They wouldn't bother her. She shoved them over out of the way.

She curled up on the floor and pillowed her head on the seat cushion. It was dark and spooky, but homelike and cozy. She flashed the light on. She could read comfortably. No one would find her. She entered another world.

The book-Rebecca liked to read books too, dozens of books that Shoo-Fly had never even heard of. She had problems too, she was one of a big family. . . . She had aunts, only two, though, one pleasant and one unpleasant . . .

It was the crow cawing loudly that brought Shoo-Fly back to life.

Jonas had been sent to find her. He thought of a quick way to locate her. He let the crow out of its pen and began to chase and tease it. The crow protested noisily, and his angry caws brought Shoo-Fly running. Pretzel was jumping and barking madly.

"Where have you *been?*" cried Punkin.

"We hunted everywhere for you," said Puddin.

Shoo-Fly put the crow back in his pen. The buggies and the aunts and the babies were all gone now. She hadn't even heard them go. Somebody had cooked supper. The family was waiting. They couldn't pray without her. She rushed to her seat on the bench, bowed her head and closed her eyes.

Her heart was beating fast under her black apron.

"Oh, God!" she prayed. "Don't let them ask me any questions!"

The World Has Open Arms

CHAPTER III

The Heart's Burden

Shoo-Fly was alone in the big kitchen. She heard a timid knock
and went to the door. There was Betty Ferguson. Nobody
had invited her.

"I came for a visit," said Betty.

Betty was dressed in T-shirt and blue jeans. Her head was a
bird's nest of curls. Shoo-Fly opened the door and Betty came in.
They stood and looked at each other. What would Mam say?

Shoo-Fly went back to her work. She was making shoo-fly pies, four of them today. Beck had lighted the gas oven and helped her mix the pastry. Now they were ready to put in.

"What are you doing?" asked Betty.

"Baking pies," said Shoo-Fly. "To sell at the pie stand on the highway."

A row of pies already baked stood on the counter.

"What's this?" Betty pointed to bread pans sitting on the back of the range. They were filled with dough set to rise. The dough was white and soft and puffy. It was rising up over the tops.

"That's bread," said Shoo-Fly. "Mam's baking bread to sell, too."

"Do you sell pies and bread?" asked Betty.

"Yes, good homemade bread," said Shoo-Fly. "I got to go to the pie stand tomorrow." As she told Betty about it, it made her feel very important.

"It looks good," said Betty. "So soft and puffy . . ." She reached out and pushed her forefinger down in the middle of each puffy loaf before Shoo-Fly could stop her. The puffs began to sink slowly and the dough went soggy.

"*Ach!*" cried Shoo-Fly. "Look now what you've done. You've ruined Mam's bread. You're not to touch it. When it goes once down, it won't come up again. It stays flat and has to be fed to the hogs."

Betty said, "Oh, does it?" She tossed her head. "How should I know?"

Bib came in first, then Beck. They both looked at the sunken loaves and scolded. Then Mam came down from upstairs. She looked at the bread and then at Shoo-Fly.

"What happened?" she asked.

Shoo-Fly pointed to Betty. "She did it. She didn't know...."

Mam frowned and said nothing. She put the shoo-fly pies in the oven and told the two girls to go outside and play.

Betty began to cry. Shoo-Fly put an arm around her. She felt sorry for her. Poor Betty didn't know any better. They went outside and saw the twins playing. They were baking cake, they said.

"I found six eggs in the hen house," said Punkin.

"We mixed them with mud . . . it makes very good cake," said Puddin.

"We put corn on the top just for fancy," said Punkin.

"So it's mud-corn cake," said Puddin.

Shoo-Fly and Betty had to laugh.

There was the crow sitting on the fence.

"Let's play with Jackie," said Shoo-Fly.

She called and the bird came and perched on her finger. She fed it some corn. The crow made talking noises.

"Say *hel-lo!*" said Shoo-Fly.

The crow cocked his head and looked at Shoo-Fly. *Hel-lo,* he cawed.

"*Hello, Jackie!*" said Shoo-Fly.

"*Hel-lo Jack-ie!*" answered the crow.

Betty laughed nervously. "I never knew a crow could talk," she said. She wasn't sure she liked the crow at all.

"Every morning he sits by my window and calls me," said

Shoo-Fly. "He tells me when it's time to get up. He won't stop until I come out and feed him."

The crow went flying up in the air. It came down and landed on the clothesline. It began to peck at the clothespins. Shoo-Fly chased it.

"Go away, Jackie! Let Mam's clothespins alone."

"What's he doing?" asked Betty.

"He likes to peck the clothespins off," said Shoo-Fly, "and hide them. He even takes our hankies and hides them!"

The crow flapped down again. He landed on Betty's head, in the middle of her curls. She screamed and fought it off. She was terrified.

"*Ach!*" cried Shoo-Fly, laughing. "You look so *strubbly*. . . ."

She chased the bird away. He flew up into the treetops. Then Rags and Hayfork came running.

"Want a ride? Want a ride?" they called. "Old Bug is waiting!"

"Take off your shoes and socks," said Sho-Fly. "It's lots more fun."

Betty did as she was told. The Amish children hated shoes and seldom wore them at home, often going barefoot even in cold weather.

Shoo-Fly and Betty ran up the bank slope to the open barn door. The barn was built on the slope of a bank. That is why it was called a bank barn. There stood an old broken-down buggy without a top. It had no shafts, no seat, only a board to sit on, but its wheels were still in running order. Rags had tied a rope to the front axle to guide it. The children climbed on and were ready to go. The twins and the dog Pretzel came too. It made a big load.

Rags gave a push and down the hill they went, laughing and screaming. Down the steep hill and into the grassy field, where Old Bug stopped. Pretzel barked loudly. They all piled out and pulled Old Bug up the hill again. Down they went over and over. It was fun.

"Oh, come on," said Shoo-Fly, getting tired. "Let's go over to Grossmama's."

Grossmama and Aunt Suzanna had been cleaning house. One of the upstairs windows was open. Jackie, the crow, had spotted the girls and now started swooping down over their heads.

"Oh, I'm scared! Make him stop!" Betty covered her head with her arms. "He'll get in my hair again. He'll scratch my eyes out!"

"He *likes* you!" said Shoo-Fly. "He won't hurt you. Don't be afraid."

"But I don't like *him!*" wailed Betty. "Make him go away."

Shoo-Fly took a broom from Grossmama's porch and waved it at the crow. He lighted on the end of the broom and made the girls laugh. Then she banged the broom on the porch post and he flew off cawing noisily.

"He's mad!" said Shoo-Fly. "He's scolding us!"

Up and around in the air flew the crow, cawing and squawking.

"Yes, well, let us alone once," said Shoo-Fly.

The crow circled around high overhead, and then, with a swoop, sailed in at the open upstairs window of Grossmama's house.

Shoo-Fly gasped. How terrible now! It was the window of the "good room," the room where all the treasures were kept.

"I must run and tell Grossmama! I must tell Aunt Suzanna, I must shoo him out of there!" Shoo-Fly ran into the house with frightened Betty at her heels.

No one was there. Where had people gone? Were they out in the garden somewhere? Shoo-Fly opened the stair door and ran up the steps. The door to the "good room" was always kept closed and the shades pulled down. But now they were up and the window open to air the room out.

There was the crow in the middle of the floor.

"Caw, caw!" he said, cocking his eye at Shoo-Fly.

"*Ach,* what a wicked bird you are!" cried Shoo-Fly. "See what you've done! Shoo out of here! Shoo on out and stay out where

you belong." She shooed and chased, the crow flapped and flopped and knocked things over. At last he found the open window and flew out, but not till after he had done a great deal of damage.

The "good room" was the place where treasures were kept. There were two handsome bureaus and two cedar chests belonging to Dat's two unmarried sisters, Aunt Suzanna and Aunt Leah. Aunt Leah was away working on a farm. The chests and bureaus were full of handmade quilts and sheets, pillowcases and towels. On the tops stood beautiful dishes and glassware, vases, cups and saucers, pitchers, water sets, serving dishes. All these things were gifts the aunts had kept since they were little girls. It was their pay for staying with their parents and taking care of them. It was their dowry for their marriage.

Aunt Suzanna's choicest treasure was a bunch of artificial fruit —grapes, peaches, lemons and bananas—that had been given her when she was ten. They were beautiful because they looked so real.

Shoo-Fly stared at them now in dismay. The crow had ruined them. He had pecked holes in the peaches, scattered the grapes and broken open the bananas. Worst of all, in his mad flight about the room, he had left a trail of broken glass and china behind him.

Shoo-Fly felt like crying.

"*Ai-y-y!* What will Grossmama say? What will Aunt Suzanna say? Now they will want to get rid of him. That's for sure!"

Betty put her arm around her.

"But it wasn't *your* fault the crow got in," she said. "Somebody left the window open . . ."

But Shoo-Fly's heart sank.

"It's my crow," she said sadly. "Nobody likes him but me."

It was an anticlimax.

Shoo-Fly had wanted to tell Betty about the "good room" and how sacred it was. The room was so elegant, it always sent shivers up and down Shoo-Fly's spine. All the furniture used to belong to dead people. None of the treasures was ever touched. They were keepsakes to be kept. Every little hanky, every dish, every vase had the name of its donor marked on it in remembrance. In the "good room," beauty and sentiment, denied in Amish living, were enshrined and held captive.

Shoo-Fly wanted to tell Betty Ferguson this. It was something important in her life. Something that Betty Ferguson had never seen or heard of. Something that "English" people did not know about.

But now it was spoiled. The "good room" had been invaded and desecrated. And by that mean old crow, Jackie! Was he really as bad and mean as everybody said?

Shoo-Fly shrugged her shoulders.

I like him anyhow, she thought. *I won't let him go. He's mine. He's the only thing I've got that nobody else wants.*

Aloud she said, "Let's go quick before Grossmama gets back."

They ran back home and there in the house yard, another calamity met their eyes. Most of Mam's nice clean washing was lying on the ground. More of Jackie's mischief. The crow had taken out all the clothespins and hid them somewhere. Jonas was right to call him a thief. Mam would be furious!

The twins came screaming, "Who took our play dishes? Who took our play dishes?"

But Shoo-Fly did not linger. Out in the barnyard, she suddenly had an idea. "Let's go horseback riding," she said.

"Oh, I'd be afraid to," said Betty.

"But you said you *liked* horses," said Shoo-Fly.

"Only in books," said Betty. "I just *love* horse books."

"We've got five horses and two mules," said Shoo-Fly. "I can hitch up a horse, feed it, harness it and ride horseback."

Betty looked at her in astonishment.

"Come, I'll show you a real horse." Shoo-Fly went in the stable and brought out old Lady. Lady was nearly twenty years old, no longer able to work. But the children loved her.

"Come, let's go for a ride!" cried Shoo-Fly.

She led Lady to the fence and climbed up on her back. Punkin and Puddin came too and climbed on behind. Betty climbed on the fence and they all pulled her up. She was up there, but sitting backwards, and they could not turn her around.

The horse was so high, it was scary to Betty. The horse was so wide, it was like being on a roof. Then the whole thing began to move and bounce up and down. Betty hung on tight. She tried not to scream, but wailing words burst from her mouth. "I want off! Take me off!" cried Betty.

Slowly at first, then round and round the barnyard the old horse

went. It was a good thing Betty was wedged in tightly, she could not possibly fall. Then—well, it wasn't so bad after all. Just when she was beginning to enjoy it, a green car drove into the barnyard.

It was Mrs. Ferguson come to take Betty home.

"Why does *she* have to come?" asked Shoo-Fly. "Can't you ever walk?" After all, Betty lived only ten minutes away.

"Let me down! Let me down!" screamed Betty. "That's Mommy!"

They all slid off and ran to the car.

Mrs. Ferguson stared in dismay. She hardly knew her own daughter. Betty's clothes were soiled and dirty. Her hair was wild and her face was black. Her feet were bare and dirty too.

"*Where* are your shoes and socks, Betty?" her mother demanded.

Shoo-Fly decided to speak up for her.

"She took them off," she said. "We hate shoes."

"I see you do," said Mrs. Ferguson, looking at all the bare, dirty feet.

"We can run faster without shoes," said Shoo-Fly.

"Betty, where are your shoes and socks?" asked Mrs. Ferguson.

It took a long time to find them. Then Betty got in the car with her mother.

"Good-by, Betty!" cried Shoo-Fly and the twins. "Come again soon."

"I never had so much fun in my whole life!" Betty called back, as the car went out the lane.

That evening Grossmama came over and reported the damage in the "good room." She said Aunt Suzanna wept over the ruined artificial fruit. Shoo-Fly told her she had found the crow inside and had shooed it out.

Everybody said the crow was bad, and Mam said she was tired of finding her washing on the ground every week and the small pieces gone. Dat said it was time to get rid of the crow. Jonas said, "Don't worry! He'll fly away one of these days and we'll never see him again." They all said such bad things about the crow that Shoo-Fly's heart sank.

What would happen to her pet?

The next day Mam took Shoo-Fly to the pie stand after school, and said she would come for her later. It was her first time at the pie stand alone. She felt very sad after Mam drove home and left

her. She tried to remember her instructions. Then she sat down
and watched the cars whizz by.

Nobody stopped. Shoo-Fly was weaving pot-holders. Beck
had showed her how. She hated to weave and the pot-holders
always ended up crooked. But Mam said she could sell them and
keep half the money. So she set to work. There was nobody to
talk to.

After a long time a car stopped. The people asked questions.
They asked her name and how old she was. They bought homemade bread. Another car stopped. A woman bought bread and
two pot-holders. Shoo-Fly took the money and put it in her
purse. It hung from its long strap over her shoulder. She opened
and shut it carefully.

The cars went zipping by. When they did not stop, Shoo-Fly
wished they would. When they did, she wished they wouldn't.
It frightened her. It was hard to talk to strangers.

Everybody wanted bread and it was soon sold out. Everybody
wanted pot-holders and she couldn't make them fast enough.
Nobody wanted pie today. The flies came and buzzed around.
Would Mam never come? And what would she say when she
saw the pies were not sold?

Now it was lonelier than ever. It was getting dark too. The
cars had turned their lights on. The headlights shone in her eyes
and blinded her. When was Mam coming? Why did Mam keep
her waiting so long? She wanted to go home. She wanted to
stay at home and never go away again.

Then all at once, two big headlights like the eyes of a monster came right toward her. Another car was going the other way, so the monster turned aside to avoid hitting it. A screech of the brakes . . . a loud crash . . . it came to a quick stop—just in time.

Shoo-Fly saw it coming, jumped back, terrified, and started to run. Anywhere, anywhere, to get away from the monster . . . Crying and sobbing she stumbled across the field. . . .

Then a man's voice spoke and a man's hand caught her by the arm.

"Don't run away," the man said. "It's all over. I didn't mean to frighten you. There's no harm done—my brakes are good. Come on back now, Shoo-Fly Girl, I won't hurt you."

She knew him at once. It was the Mystery Man from Massachusetts, who liked shoo-fly pie so much. He was the one who had given her that terrible nickname. Now he had almost run over her. If she had not run . . .

Then she looked. The pie stand stood where it always stood. It was not hurt at all. Nothing was disturbed. The big black monster's headlights threw a bright light on everything—on all the pies and cakes that nobody wanted.

"Well, Shoo-Fly Girl, that was a close shave!" said the man calmly. "That crazy driver was heading straight for me and I had to get out of his way. I'm sorry I frightened you."

He pointed to the pies. "How's business today—good? 'Bout time for you to go home, isn't it? Nobody here with you today? How are the pies, good?"

Shoo-Fly could not answer any of his questions. She was still white and shaken. Why didn't Mam come and take her and the pies and cakes home?

"I'll take everything," the man said, but Shoo-Fly did not hear.

He put some bills in her hand and started to put the pies in a box in his car.

Then Shoo-Fly heard the sound of a horse's hoofs and the next minute Mam got out of her buggy. Shoo-Fly ran to her mother's arms and burst into tears. "He tried to run over me!" she cried.

The man talked to Mam, explaining everything. He ended up saying, "I bought her out."

"*Ach,* but . . ." Mrs. Fisher began. "You must have a big family, to eat all those pies and cakes. . . ."

The man turned toward her. His face had a stricken look.

"Yes—big family . . ." he said.

He started up his car and drove away.

"Don't make me go again! Don't make me go again!" begged Shoo-Fly all the way home.

The world was full of peril and risk, temptation and evil. All her life, Shoo-Fly had been warned of the dangers of worldliness. From the safe and quiet world of her home, she had taken her first step outside, and she did not like what she saw there. She crept home, hurt and bewildered.

Then another blow came, worse than the first. It came close, not striking her directly, but her brother Jonas, and that was almost the same as herself. For he was the favorite of all her brothers and sisters, the only one who understood her.

Dat and Jonas and Rags had gone over to Uncle Chris's to help fill the silo with green corn. The farm seemed empty and lifeless without them. In the late afternoon Shoo-Fly went out to gather the eggs. Some of the hens liked to lay in the barn, so she went in to look for eggs. Shoo-Fly could not climb up on the rafters now and jump down in the soft hay any more. All the upper part was filled with drying tobacco.

She walked around slowly. Becky Green-Eyes and her kittens came up mewing, so she got some milk and fed them. Now and then she found an egg and put it in her basket. The whole place was quiet. Off in the field she could hear the crows cawing and knew that Jackie must be with them.

Suddenly a strange sound met her ears. She stood still and listened. Was she dreaming? Was it music? Where was it coming from? It was very soft, and sometimes it nearly died away. Then it came on louder annd sweeter again. Was it . . . could it be . . . a radio? Miss Weber had one at school, the only one Shoo-Fly had ever heard. Amish families did not have them. The Bishop told them they were not necessary.

The music was light and lively. It made Shoo-Fly feel happy, almost like dancing on her toes. *Where* was it coming from? It must be *secret* music, hidden away somewhere. Forgetting about the eggs, Shoo-Fly searched. She knew all the dark corners and out-of-the-way hiding places. She crept about quietly, in the harness room and out, in the stable and out, in the egg room, the granary, and then in the old carriage shed. It was like a game, playing now "hot," now "cold." She felt herself getting warmer and warmer, as she came up to the old broken buggy. It was Old Bug, the one the children played with. A big canvas had been thrown over the half-broken frame, to make a shelter. She crept around to the back and looked in.

There sat Jonas, big fifteen-year-old Jonas, huddled in a heap. On the seat of the buggy was a radio, set on the floor.

"*Ach!*" cried Shoo-Fly. "So it's you! I found you once."

"Sh! Sh!" said Jonas, finger to his lips. "Why do *you* have to come here and spoil everything?"

"I . . . I heard the music and . . ." began Shoo-Fly.

"Well now, clear out! Get going! Go on away and don't come around here again!"

"But I thought you went to Uncle Chris's to help fill the silo," said Shoo-Fly.

"I did and I worked and I came away," said Jonas. "They've got all the help they need without me."

Shoo-Fly pointed to the forbidden radio.

"Where did you get it?" she asked in a whisper.

"I *borrowed* it," said Jonas. "And don't you go tell on me!"

Shoo-Fly shook her head. She and Jonas were friends. They liked each other. She could count on Jonas more than on any of her other brothers or sisters. She could not be disloyal. Jonas was a big tease, but most of the time he was good to her. She climbed up in the buggy and sat down.

"What will Dat say if he finds out?" she asked.

"He won't say much, he'll just smash it."

"What will the Bishop say?" she whispered.

"I won't tell him," said Jonas.

"But if he finds out?" said Shoo-Fly.

"He won't, unless some little squirt squeals on me," said Jonas.

"On that one at school last year I heard all about space and

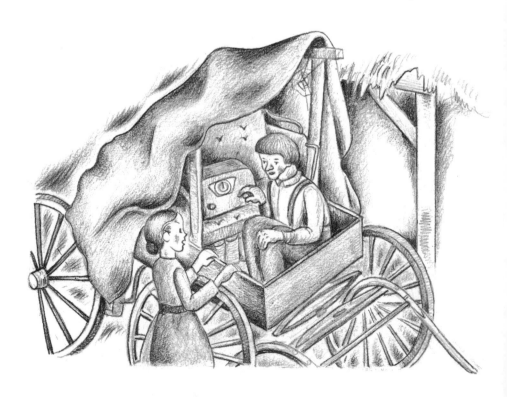

rockets and missiles. . . ." He turned the knob and the tune changed to a loud noisy one. He tuned it lower. "That's *jazz!*" he said with a grin.

"*Ach!* I don't like it!" said Shoo-Fly, frightened. "Turn it off! It hurts my ears terrible!"

"It's all the rage . . ." said Jonas, "Bill Ferguson tells me."

Shoo-Fly knew that Betty had an older brother named Bill. "Did you borrow it from Bill?" she asked.

Jonas closed his lips tight. "I'm not telling," he said. Then he looked at his sister and blurted out, "Sometimes I wish I wasn't Amish at all. I *like* TV and radios and cars!"

"*Ach,* Jonas!" gasped Shoo-Fly. "*Don't* say that!"

"It's true," said Jonas. "I can't help it."

"Where have you seen TV?" asked Shoo-Fly.

"At a tavern in town," said Jonas. "Bill took me. Bill wants me to go away with him . . . to Canada, maybe. . . . He has some rich relatives living there . . . we could do as we please. . . . There are no bishops up there."

"*Ach,* Jonas!" cried Shoo-Fly in distress. "*Don't* say that!"

Jonas had not meant to tell her at all. But she was his trusting friend, and he had to tell somebody. He felt better after he had blurted it out. Then, even in the dim light of the shed, he saw the shocked look on his sister's face and it frightened him.

"Oh, *shucks!*" he said. "Forget it! I'm not going, don't get so scared. It's just that sometimes I *wish* I could!"

He had turned the radio off now.

"Don't tell anybody where I keep it," said Jonas.

"I won't," said Shoo-Fly. Then she had an idea. "If . . . if you like music . . ." she began, "why don't you get a mouth organ instead? The Bishop says harmonicas are O.K."

"Huh!" snorted Jonas. "Kid stuff! Who wants one of them?"

"But you can play pretty tunes on it . . ." said Shoo-Fly.

Somehow she wanted to help her brother, but how?

"Take your eggs and go in the house," said Jonas. "I'm going back to Uncle Chris's. This is *our* secret now. Will you promise me you won't tell?"

Shoo-Fly nodded, her face serious.

There was no one around as she slowly made her way to the back door. But her heart was heavy with the burden that Jonas had placed there.

CHAPTER IV

A Godly Child

"Oh! We're going to Grossdawdy Yoder's!"

Shoo-Fly danced around on her tippy toes. What fun that would be! To take Cousin Eli's new pony cart over! Maybe Eli would give her a ride!

Shoo-Fly was glad when she heard that church would be held next Sunday at Uncle Dave's. The Amish people had no church buildings. They took turns holding church meetings in different

63

homes. It was a big event to have church held at your house.

Of course it meant work, too. There was always something to take the joy out of life. But no need to worry about that now.

On Saturday, Mam and Jonas and Reuben and Shoo-Fly climbed into the buggy. The others stayed at home. Dat hitched Eli's pony cart on behind the buggy and told Jonas to keep his eye on it. Jonas and Shoo-Fly rode in the back with the curtain rolled up.

They had not gone far when they saw a black shadow fly overhead. Back and forth over the buggy it went, back and forth over Skipper's head, darting down and then up.

"Ach, it's Jackie!" cried Shoo-Fly. "I let him out of his pen and forgot to put him back. He likes to stay out and fly around."

"He likes to fly away," said Jonas. "Some day he'll be gone."

"Oh no," said Shoo-Fly. "He's tame. He won't leave me."

"Did you feed him?" asked Jonas.

"No, I forgot."

"Crows can't ever get enough to eat," said Jonas. "They're worse than hogs. The more you feed them, the more they want."

"Jackie's going right along with us!" cried Shoo-Fly. "Hi, Jackie, come here! Come, sit on my finger and I'll give you a ride!"

"Don't call him," said Jonas. "Better let him go home. If he comes along, he'll get lost and you'll never see him again."

They turned into the highway and the crow disappeared.

"I think Jackie got tired and went home," said Shoo-Fly.

Shoo-Fly's mother was a Yoder and one of seven sisters.

Grossmama and Grossdawdy Yoder lived at their son Dave's, near Bird-in-Hand. Grossmama Yoder was an invalid and had a hired girl to take care of her. The grandparents lived in the Grossdawdy house. Uncle Dave and Aunt Sadie lived in the other half of the double house. They had five children, Eli the oldest, then three little girls and baby Jonny.

Today all the seven aunts, Uncle Dave's sisters, were there to help get Aunt Sadie's house ready for church. There was no time for fooling. Everybody was put to work. Aunt Martha, the oldest, was the boss. She could not tolerate laziness. She gave orders right and left.

Shoo-Fly put her head in at the back door. Everything was in a hubbub. Rugs were rolled up and chairs pushed into corners. Two aunts stood on chairs washing windows. Two more cleaned stoves and polished them. All the folding doors between downstairs rooms had been removed, others taken off their hinges.

"Suzanna!" cried Aunt Martha. "Take these babies out from underfoot. Keep them in the yard."

Shoo-Fly hated baby-sitting, but she took the children out.

No chance for a ride in the pony cart today. She could see that. Even Eli hadn't had a chance to look at it. He was busy like everybody else. He and Jonas and Reuben and other boy cousins were hard at work. They were whitewashing all the fences. Then the stables had to be cleaned and swept. Everything had to be spick and span for church tomorrow.

Out the back door came Aunt Martha. Shoo-Fly hated to see her come. Didn't she have enough to do inside?

"Suzanna, get busy and rake up all the leaves!" she ordered.

It was fall and leaves were coming down fast. The baby cousins were too little to help. All they could do was squawl. Beck and Bib had been left at home to do Saturday cleaning there. Shoo-Fly had to keep an eye on the babies and do the raking herself. It was no fun at all.

She had just finished when Aunt Martha came out again. She was not satisfied.

"Look what a mess!" she said. "Look at the leaves you've left! Pick up every single one in your fingers—every single one!"

Shoo-Fly's mouth fell open. "But the wind . . ." she began. "It keeps blowing them down from the trees. . . ."

The wind did not bother Aunt Martha.

"Every single leaf!" she said, shaking her finger at Shoo-Fly.

"Do you want me to stand every single blade of grass up straight too?" asked Shoo-Fly. But she said it under her breath, so Aunt Martha would not hear. Nobody ever talked back to Aunt Martha.

And so it went on, work, work, work. No fun at all. No pony-cart ride, not even a chance to ask Eli for a ride.

No chance to see Grossdawdy Yoder either. Where was he? Had he gone off for the day to get away from all the women, or was he hiding somewhere? Shoo-Fly dropped her rake and ran over to his toyshop to see.

Yes, Grossdawdy had a toyshop. He said he was retired now, too old to do farming. Let son Dave do the work. He would take life easy, but not just loaf, no, no. He had to have something to do, and he liked to hammer and saw. So he had cleaned out the old chicken house across the lane and made it into a toyshop.

It was a fascinating place and Shoo-Fly liked to go there. Grossdawdy made toys to sell to tourists. He jigsawed out toy horses and lions and pigs and cows, and painted them. He made toy barns and barnyards. He made not only toys but big birdhouses.

Grossdawdy loved purple martins. It was he who had put up the four martin houses on high posts in the Fishers' barnyard. He had four more in his own barnyard. Grossdawdy knew all about martins. He told stories about the one with the white breast that came back year after year.

Today the door to the toyshop was locked. Shoo-Fly could not get in. She peeped through the window. No one was there. Where was Grossdawdy anyhow?

Back in the barnyard, she saw the men coming in wagons, bringing the long benches for the people to sit on at church tomorrow. They took them into the house.

Then it was time to go home. It had been no fun at all.

But the next day, Sunday, promised better. Shoo-Fly awoke excited and happy.

Sunday meant getting up at five-thirty and doing chores before daylight. It meant eating a hurried breakfast, then helping the little ones get ready. The boys had to be washed and combed and dressed, shoes put on and tied. The twins had to be washed, hair combed and braided, capes and white aprons pinned and caps put on and tied. Pins got lost and could not be found. It took so many pins—each apron took five, each cape five more . . . where did the pins go to, anyway?

But at last everybody was off, two buggies full. Just as they were starting, Shoo-Fly saw Jackie flying overhead. She heard him cawing noisily. *Maybe he wants to go to church,* she thought. Then she put the thought away, knowing how wicked it was. The country road was full of buggies, all going in the same direction. Shoo-Fly and the twins sat in the back of Grossmama Fisher's buggy. The rear curtain was down and they could not see a thing. It was like being cooped up in prison, a long, long neverending drive.

At last old Sonny Boy stopped, backed around, and they all got out at Grossdawdy Yoder's. A large flock of birds flew overhead, but no one noticed. Soon the excitement began. Uncle Dave's place looked as neat as a pin, not a blade of grass out of place. A procession of Amish buggies was coming down the lane, others were already there. People were coming from all directions. Everybody would see how clean and neat Uncle Dave's place was. Not a single leaf on the lawn. The wind must have stopped blowing. Shoo-Fly smiled in smug satisfaction.

The house was half full already, the long benches all in place. All the bearded men left their big black felt hats on the porch and sat together on one side, all the white-capped women and girls on the other side. The two big rooms opened up together made it seem as big as a real church. The stove and sideboard, which could not be moved, had been discreetly covered with dark cloth pinned tightly down. Nothing wordly must intrude. The dark green shades were pulled halfway down in a neat line. Aunt Sadie's African violets sat in a row on high shelves across the windows, blooming gaily, unafraid. The peaked clock on the high shelf above the fancy pincushions was not afraid to tick and even strike when necessary. But all else was very quiet. Sunday was a solemn occasion.

Sunday meant seeing a lot of people. There were a hundred and sixty in this district, counting the children, and they were all there except the sick. Church meant shaking hands with everybody. Shoo-Fly felt her hand go limp and thought it would drop off. She was glad to sit down at last.

Just in time. Here came the long line of boys, Eli, Jonas and Reuben and too many others to count. They had had to take care of all the horses, unhitch them from their buggies and put them in the barn. Now the boys marched in, single file, removed their

hats and took their places behind the men.   Soon in came the
Bishop, the deacon and the three ministers.   They sat down in
big rocking chairs reserved for them.   They had backs to rest on.
Singing, a soft whining chant, began and kept on.

Shoo-Fly sat with Mam, who had Aunt Sadie's baby on her lap,
and the twins, on the women's side.   The twins looked as nice as
Shoo-Fly did, with white Sunday aprons and white caps on.   Only
on Sunday did they wear white.   What's more, their dresses were
pink, a lovely pink.   This was quite a change from school dresses,
which were always in dark colors.   It made Sunday a very special
day.

The little boys, Henry or Hayfork and Sammy, sat with Dat
across the room.   All the young fathers took care of toddlers, leaving the babies to the young mothers.

The service began early, at eight-thirty, and moved slowly, in-
evitably along.   Hymn-singing came at intervals between preaching, praying and testimony.   The first sermon was short, the
second one long.   Shoo-Fly listened.   Words, German words
like *ewigkeit* and *himmel,* washed over her as the men's voices
rose and fell.   Through it all ran a comforting, homelike din—
babies crying, children fussing and feeding, being taken in and
out, things dropping and being picked up, children walking out
and coming back right under the Bishop's nose and gesturing
arms.   The hands on the clock on the mantel seemed to stand
still if watched, but sometimes the clock growled and struck the
hour, nine, ten, then eleven . . .

Most of the younger children were barefoot.   Bare feet did not mean poverty nor carelessness, but comfort. Shoo-Fly's shoes were left in the buggy. Now with her bare toes she opened Mam's little covered basket sitting on the floor. It held all sorts of surprises. Pretty "hankies" to make "mice" or "cradle and baby" out of, cookies to nibble on, pretzels to chew, a spool rattle for Aunt Sadie's baby and a little storybook. Shoo-Fly got it out and read it in a whisper to Punkin and Puddin.

Everything was going fine, when suddenly a loud noise was heard. It came from outside, a tremendous squawking, close at hand. Birds were flying close over the barnyard, coming in closer up to the tree by the house. Were they martins? No, the martins had gone south long ago. Starlings? Maybe. A man across the room pulled the shade up behind him and looked out. Shoo-Fly stretched her neck to see. The Bishop went on shouting, as if

trying to drown out the clamor of the birds.

Baby Jonny began to wail. Mam whispered to Shoo-Fly, telling her to take him out to the kitchen and get him a drink of water. Shoo-Fly got up, baby in arms, and began stumbling over women's feet. She went out to the porch. The yard was full of birds.

"See the birds, Jonny!" she whispered, pointing. Jonny laughed.

They were crows, black crows. Shoo-Fly's heart skipped a beat. Was Jackie there among them? Of course not, Jackie was safe back at home. They were making a terrible noise as if it was not Sunday at all. The Bishop did not like noise on Sunday, but the birds did not care. They cawed and cawed. They flew out and back. They acted as if they were holding a meeting of their own. Other Amish children sneaked out to the porch and watched smiling. One big crow seemed to be the master voice. He gave the others orders. Was he preaching to them? Shoo-Fly wondered. He chased them away, one by one.

He was left all alone in the tree. Did he quiet down then? No! He cawed louder than ever. Was he trying to out-caw the Bishop?

The Bishop did not like it. He stopped his sermon, spoke to a man beside him and the man went out. The man waved his arms and yelled, but the crow would not go away. It kept on making raucous noises. The man got a stick and waved it, but the crow would not go away.

When the service was over, everybody got up and stretched.

The women brought cold food to the long tables. They put sliced bread, pickles, Lebanon bologna, cheese in square hunks and jams on the table. The older men sat down to eat in the front room, the older women in the kitchen. Then the younger men and the younger women, and at last the children. Shoo-Fly was hungry. Her arm reached out to get what she could—bread, cheese, bologna and pickles. Then she ran out to play. The crows were gone now.

All the children enjoyed being turned loose again. They piled benches on top of each other to make slides. The little girls slid down on their tummies, right on their pretty white Sunday aprons. Nobody scolded them. The small boys made a slide of their own. They slid down all together, landing in a laughing heap at the bottom. Nobody scolded them either.

The older men sat quietly under the large shade tree and talked. The Bishop was in the center. Everybody listened to what he had to say.

Then out of the blue sky down came a crow. It was the same bad black crow that had disturbed the service. It flew down close over the men's heads. It interrupted their conversation. The Bishop took off his hat and waved it. He tried to shoo the crow away, but it would not go. The other men shooed it, still it would not go. It seemed to be very tame. It seemed to like the Bishop.

Shoo-Fly ran closer to see. Was it, could it be Jackie? Could Jackie have followed the buggy all the way over to Grossdawdy's house? The next minute the crow was on her hand.

Ach, now, it *was* Jackie! And she forgot to feed him this morning. Had he come so far to get some dinner? *Oh dear, oh dear . . .*

The Bishop was coming toward her. What would he do? What could *she* do? Trembling, she did not know which way to turn. "Go away, Jackie!" The bird now sat on her outstretched hand. "Shoo! Shoo! Go on home now. Stop bothering us! It's *Sunday,* don't you know that, Jackie?"

The Bishop came closer. All the children stopped their play and stood silent. The crow flew up in the air. The Bishop patted Shoo-Fly on the head.

"What a pleasure to see such a godly child!" he said. "I saw you entertaining the little ones. Good girl."

"*Ach!*" cried Shoo-Fly, looking up at him in surprise. "I

thought you were going to scold my crow."

"No," said the Bishop. "God made the birds, even ugly noisy birds like the crows. Does this crow belong to you?"

Shoo-Fly nodded.

The crow had settled on her shoulder now. She could not speak.

"What a fine pet!" said the Bishop.

Then he went away. That was all.

After the Bishop and the deacon and the church members went away, only the family was left. They were not in a hurry to go home. They sat around and visited.

Grossdawdy Yoder came up to the little girls and said, "Come, I have something to show you."

Shoo-Fly and the twins followed him. Grossdawdy was a great one for secrets and surprises. He led them to the toyshop. The toyshop was always locked on Sundays, but he took the key from his pocket and unlocked the door.

"I have a surprise for you," he said.

He opened the door, and there on a low table right inside stood a dollhouse. A big beautiful, two-story dollhouse, with roof and windows and two chimneys and everything. The girls looked with big eyes, in silence.

"And you say noddings?" Grossdawdy laughed until his white beard shook. "You got noddings to say?"

"Did you make it?" asked Punkin.

"Who is it for?" asked Puddin.

"So that's what you want to know!" laughed Grossdawdy. "I fool you this time—it's *not* for you! A man came, a tourist, he say he is from Massachusetts. He want I should make it for . . ."

"He got little girls?" asked Punkin.

"*Ja*, two little girls, he tell me," said Grossdawdy.

"It's nice," said Puddin.

"I like it," said Punkin.

Even the twins were learning self-denial.

Shoo-Fly had never played much with dolls. There were always babies to be tended. She looked the dollhouse over carefully. One side was open, so she could see into all the rooms above and below. Two stairways had been put in, but something was wrong. At the tops of the steps, there were no holes in the floor. So the stairs were useless.

"Susie, what are you thinking?" asked Grossdawdy, putting his arm around her shoulder.

"The stairs, they go nowhere," said Shoo-Fly.

Grossdawdy roared with laughter.

Then she asked, "Did you say the man was from Massachusetts?"

"*Ja*," said Grossdawdy. "So he said."

Shoo-Fly thought of the Mystery Man at the pie stand. It couldn't be the same person. There were many tourists from Massachusetts.

They went out and Grossdawdy locked the door again.

"Now we go to see Grossmama," he said, leading the way into the big stone house.

The children followed and came to the bedroom. Grossmama Yoder was sitting in an easy chair. She was pale and thin. She looked at them and smiled, but she could not talk. Awe-struck, the children said a few words and went out.

Then Eli came bustling up from the barn, looking very important. "Who wants a ride in my new pony cart?" he asked.

"I do! I do!" cried the twins and Shoo-Fly.

Round the corner of the barn came Eli's pony hitched up to the new pony cart. He took the littlest cousins for a ride first, down the lane and back. Then he took the older ones. Eli was very grand and very generous, showing off his new pony cart. Eli kept on urging his pony Buster to go faster and faster. Eli thought it was fun to show off, even if it was Sunday.

Shoo-Fly had to wait a long time for her turn. Then she got

in with Reuben and Henry.   Buster started out the lane and came
back, as usual.   But he did not stop—he kept on going faster.
Back in the barnyard, he darted from the path, dashed across the
vegetable garden and flower beds, bumped into the newly white-
washed fence, then started around the springhouse, flying around
corners on two wheels.   Eli thought it was a big joke and kept
slapping the reins.   *Oh, what a ride. . . .*

   Eli began shouting and the children began laughing, it was so
funny.   The pony had never done anything like this before.   Then
they were crying out with fright, as they hung on for dear life.
Was the pony running away?   Buster was a quiet old pony.   He
had never galloped in his life.   Now the new pony cart went
bouncing across the ruts in the tobacco field, jolting up and down
behind a wild-eyed, galloping pony.

Uncle Dave and Dat came tearing behind. The women and children at the house began screaming. First Sammy went tumbling off, then Henry, but Shoo-Fly hung on.

Then she saw what had happened. She saw the black wings flapping over her head. She heard the loud caws of the mean old crow. Was Jackie bent on Sunday mischief? Was Jackie as mean as everyone said he was? Was she the only one who liked having a crow for a pet?

Down in front of the pony's eyes the crow darted, then up over its head, landing between its ears, all the time cawing and scaring the poor pony half to death. No wonder old Buster ran away!

Then at last the cart was stopped, but not before the hind hoofs of the pony had struck cousin Eli in the head. The men got there, stopped the crazed pony and picked Eli up off the ground, a stream of blood running from his forehead.

They left the cart where it was. One of the men unfastened the harness and took Buster back to the barn. Shoo-Fly still held onto the sides of the pony cart. Her knuckles were white, she was holding so tight. She sat there for a while after the others left. She saw Henry and Sammy get up and run back, none the worse for their tumbles. But Eli was killed—she was sure of that. And her conscience smote her. She had said and thought so many bad things about Eli. And now he was dead.

She felt something on her shoulder.

She looked. There was Jackie, the mean old crow who had caused all the trouble.

He cocked his eye at her and said, *"Caw, caw, caw!"*

It was a sad home-going after a happy day.

Uncle Dave had to get a non-Amish neighbor with a car to take Eli to the hospital. Eli was still unconscious. Nobody knew how badly he was hurt. Grossmama Fisher and Aunt Suzanna talked about it all the way home.

Shoo-Fly cried till she thought her heart would break.

The World Is Fear and Danger

CHAPTER V

Venture into the Unknown

"W ill Eli get well?"

Every day Shoo-Fly asked the question which no one could answer. All they knew was that he was still at the hospital.

In spite of the accident, Shoo-Fly still loved her pet crow Jackie, and fed him regularly. She talked to him and he talked back. But now he never sat on her finger or her shoulder any more. She could never hold him. He was getting too big for that. Was he getting ready to fly off and never come back again, the way Jonas said?

One day, Grossmama asked Shoo-Fly to take a ride with her. She did not ask the twins, she said it was Shoo-Fly's turn. She did not say where she was going. Grossmama was very independent. She never told anyone. She just went. She might be going to see Great-Grossmama at Uncle John's, or to the store, or to the doctor, or to pick up Aunt Suzanna at the gift shop.

Shoo-Fly climbed in the buggy and sat on the seat. Then Grossmama stepped up briskly.

"I can get in without hitting my head," Grossmama said. "Every time I ride in a car, I bump my head even though I am so little. They make cars so low now."

"*Grossmama,* do *you* ride in *cars?*" asked Shoo-Fly, astonished.

"*Ach, ja,* now and then, when I have to."

"But Mam scolded me and told me not to ride in the Fergusons' car any more," said Shoo-Fly. "Once Mrs. Ferguson brought me home from school."

"That wasn't necessary, was it?" said Grossmama. "You can still walk, can't you?"

"*Ja,* but . . . but cars are safer than buggies," said Shoo-Fly.

"Who said that?"

"Mrs. Ferguson," said Shoo-Fly.

A car whizzed up from behind and Shoo-Fly jumped.

"No need to be afraid," said Grossmama. "The cars won't hit us. I've got a mirror, I can see when they come up behind. We've got as much right on the road as the cars have."

Another car boomed by. Shoo-Fly jumped again.

"I can see it! I can see it coming," cried Grossmama. "I keep out of their way." She slapped the lines and said, "Come on now, Sonny Boy."

"But Elam Esh got hit by a car, and his buggy got smashed and he had to buy a new one," said Shoo-Fly. "Dat is making it now."

"Elam always was a careless man," said Grossmama. "I've known him since he wore diapers. Giddap, Sonny Boy."

"Sonny Boy's slow," said Shoo-Fly. "Why don't you get a faster horse, Grossmama?"

"Why do I want to go fast?" said Grossmama. "I've got all the time in the world. Sonny Boy's a Grossmama horse, nice and tame. He's supposed to go slow."

"Couldn't you buy a faster horse at the Horse Sale in New Holland?" asked Shoo-Fly.

"At the Horse Sale you never know what you are getting," said Grossmama, "even if they let you try the horse first. I bought Sonny Boy from Gideon Glick, an Amish farmer I can trust. Sonny Boy's nine years old and he's tame. I paid two hundred dollars for him."

"It will be nice when Jonas gets a horse," said Shoo-Fly.

"Jonas will want a three-year-old, a pacer, and harness with all the trimmings," chuckled Grossmama. "Mother-of-pearl rings, colored rosettes and white snaps to make a big show. *Ach,* well, boys are only young once! He will settle down soon enough, once he gets a horse and a courting buggy."

"Do you like to ride in cars, Grossmama?" asked Shoo-Fly.

"Once I rode to Akron in a Mennonite car," laughed Gross-mama. "We went so fast I couldn't keep my bonnet on. I couldn't see what crops they were growing in the fields. There was so much waste land up there. The farmers don't farm as we do here. We had to stop and buy gas twice. It cost five dollars for that trip!"

She paused. Then she added, "In my buggy all day I can ride, and it won't cost me a cent."

They went riding on and on. There was something very comforting about riding in a buggy—the *clop, clop, clop* of Sonny Boy's hoofs, and the chance to see all the crops, each tree, each fence and creek and windmill, and each house and barnyard, especially when you knew who lived there. The ride was a long one and at last they turned down a lane and Shoo-Fly knew where she was.

They had come to Grossdawdy Yoder's and Uncle Dave's. Several dogs and the little girls came running out to meet them. Then came Aunt Sadie with baby Jonny from the house, and Grossdawdy from his toyshop. They crowded round the buggy. Grossmama said they would not get out. They were just taking a buggy ride and must go right home again.

"Did Eli get well?" asked Shoo-Fly.

"Where is Eli?" asked Grossmama.

Aunt Sadie turned to the little girls. "Tell Eli to come out." They ran indoors.

Soon a boy came out the door, a strange-looking boy, not like Eli at all. What had happened to him? Didn't they feed him enough at the hospital? Or had he grown several inches?

"Why, Eli, is it you?" asked Shoo-Fly.

"*Ach* now, I don't know you!" cried Grossmama Fisher.

"Why, Eli!" cried Shoo-Fly. *"You're an English boy!"*

"Eli's an English boy! Eli's an English boy!" chanted his sisters.

Everybody laughed. Eli's hair had been cut short at the hospital. The blow of the pony's hoof had struck the top of his head right in his hair. So all his long Amish bobbed hair had been cut and the top of his head shaved. A bald Amish boy was something unusual. No wonder Eli had gone into hiding.

He did not like to be laughed at.

"It's not my fault," he grumbled. "It was the mean old crow of yours. . . ." He glared at Shoo-Fly.

Grossmama Fisher spoke up. "I can see that Eli is getting well again. His temper is as bad as ever!"

They all laughed again. Then the visitors said good-by.

Grossmama drove off and they waved to Eli. Shoo-Fly felt relieved. At least Eli was not killed. He was still very much alive. Jackie had not done such a terrible thing, after all. Now she could keep him. Shoo-Fly felt happy again.

One day Betty Ferguson came and asked Mam if Shoo-Fly could go to her house for a visit. Mam said she could and the two girls walked out the lane and up the road together.

It was her first visit to a non-Amish home and Shoo-Fly hardly knew what to expect. Of course they spoke English, the way the children did at school. It was nice to speak English and to read it in books. All the "English" people spoke it. People all over Pennsylvania spoke it and all over the United States and all over the world, Miss Weber said. Shoo-Fly was glad she could speak it too. Mam insisted they speak Dutch at home, but whenever you left home, English was the thing!

Shoo-Fly went in Betty's house and looked around. It was very different from an Amish home. She stared with big eyes. There was so much to see.

The rooms were small and very crowded. There were lace curtains and soft carpets and pictures on the wall, and books and magazines and framed photographs looking at you from every direction. Also there was noise—the TV and a radio were blaring, and there was a piano to play. . . . The telephone began to ring and kept on ringing. . . . The whole house was an assault on her eyes and her ears.

"What do you want to do?" Betty asked.

"I don't know," said Shoo-Fly.

"Let's look at TV," said Betty.

They squatted on cushions on the floor and looked at the flickering screen. Shoo-Fly could see shadows like people darting back and forth, and she heard loud shouting noises. But she could not tell what it was all about. Then men began pointing guns and banging. It confused, then alarmed her. She suddenly remembered.

She jumped up. "I don't want to see it," she told Betty.

"Why ever not?" said Betty. "I just love it."

"It's not allowed. . . ." said Shoo-Fly. "I'm Amish."

But Betty could hardly hear through the noisy din. The telephone rang and Betty got up to answer it. Shoo-Fly listened to the one-sided conversation. She had never talked on the telephone in her life.

"It's my brother Bill," Betty said. "Do you want to talk to him, Suzanna? Come and say hello to him."

"*Ach,* no!" cried Suzanna, frightened. "I don't want to."

Betty hung up the receiver.

"Mommy," she called, "Bill says he won't be home for supper. He wouldn't tell where he was going."

Then Mr. Ferguson came in. "You girls come on outside," he said. Mrs. Ferguson bustled in from the kitchen.

"Put your bonnet back on, Suzanna," she said. "Ain't she *cute!*"

Outside, before she realized it, Mr. Ferguson pointed a camera at her and snapped her photograph. It happened quickly.

"Don't do that!" cried Suzanna, unhappily. "It's not allowed."

"Just one more," said Mr. Ferguson. "Betty, put your arm around Suzanna's waist."

Suzanna could not stop him. There was nothing she could do. She felt like crying, but held back the tears. Why had she come here? She must get away quickly and go home.

But Mrs. Ferguson had supper ready and Betty placed a chair for her. It was getting dark, so she turned on the electric light. The click of the switch was too sudden and the flash of the light too harsh. Shoo-Fly blinked. She took her bonnet off and sat down. She looked at Betty's hands. She had red paint on her fingernails. She looked at Betty's lips. She had red lipstick on her lips. She folded her own hands in her lap to pray, but they began eating at once.

"I made *schnitz und knepp* just for you, Suzanna," said Mrs. Ferguson. "It's cooked with ham the way you do, but we call it dried apple dumplings."

Shoo-Fly took a few mouthfuls. Why had she come? She put down her fork. She tried hard not to cry. "I want to go home," she said.

"Why, the poor child's homesick! Can you imagine?" said Mrs. Ferguson. "Betty, can't you do something to amuse her, to make her stop crying?"

Betty left the table and brought out a string of red beads.

"You can have it," she said.

But Shoo-Fly did not even look. She buried her face in her hands.

"I guess I'd better take her home," said Mrs. Ferguson.

"No—don't *take* her," said Mr. Ferguson. "Let her go."

"That's right," said Mrs. Ferguson. "She's got legs to walk, her mother said. But I hate to see her go off down the road alone, crying. It's getting dark—but what can we do?"

Betty turned to Suzanna.

"I wanted you to stay all night with me," she said. "But I don't suppose you want to. . . ."

Shoo-Fly shook her head.

Drying her tears, Shoo-Fly ran all the way home. She felt like a bird let out of a cage. She got there just in time to put the supper dishes in the cupboard, after the twins had dried them. Home was a haven, a shelter. The everyday routine made it home.

"Betty asked me to stay all night," she told the girls.

"Why didn't you?" asked Beck.

Shoo-Fly tossed her head. "I didn't take my nightgown."

Then she went on. "Mrs. Ferguson said I look cute in my bonnet." She might as well tell the worst. All her horror was gone now. She was filled with daring. "Mr. Ferguson took a picture of me wearing my bonnet!"

"Suzanna! No!" cried Mam. "You didn't let him?"

Shoo-Fly hung her head. "He never asked me. He just took it."

Dat spoke up. "How could she stop him?" he asked. He turned to Suzanna and repeated what she knew already. "We do not approve of photographs. It is not our way. We are Amish."

Shoo-Fly told about things in the Fergusons' home, the lace curtains, the electric lights that hurt your eyes, the television that jumped and the telephone that jangled. The others listened. Jonas smiled broadly.

"It's high time for you to get away from home now once," said Jonas, "to see how other people do things. The Fergusons are nice people. I like them."

Dat looked at Jonas sharply, but said nothing.

It was time for bed, foot-washing time. Beck brought the foot tub with warm water. One by one the children stepped into it and washed their feet, the older girls helping. They put on their nightgowns.

Dat got out his big book and the children crowded round. He read from the Bible and they all sang a hymn together. Shoo-Fly folded her hands in peace. How good it was to be home again.

Betty Ferguson had offered her the key to another world, but she was not like Jonas. She was reluctant to enter it.

Every day Shoo-Fly watched Jonas. Was he going to go away without telling anybody? What was that he said about "getting away from home"? It seemed as if Shoo-Fly would never get a chance to talk to Jonas alone. There was always somebody around. In a big family there was no privacy at all. Everybody knew everybody else's business. Jonas felt the same way about it. He liked to go off and be by himself whenever he could. It was hidden away in Old Bug that she found him again.

The radio was playing softly, but Jonas did not listen. He wanted somebody to talk to. He talked about going to Canada again. He said three boys were going to hitchhike and camp along the way.

To Shoo-Fly it sounded like make-believe.

"What will you eat?" she asked.

"We'll pick berries and fruit for people," said Jonas.

"But winter will soon be here, and it's cold in Canada," she said.

"We'll get jobs," said Jonas.

"Where will you sleep?" asked Shoo-Fly.

"Up in a tree," said Jonas.

Shoo-Fly laughed. Now she was sure he was joking. "You'll fall down!"

But Jonas sounded serious. "Bill wants to leave home. He says his father's mean to him. I've got to help him. He's a nice boy, even if he is English. He's nice or he wouldn't have given me this radio. They've got two other better ones and a TV."

"You'll have to have money to go on a trip," said Shoo-Fly.

"I've got some," said Jonas.

"But you give your money to Dat, don't you, to save for you?"

"I don't give him all of it," said Jonas. "I'm old enough to have some spending money of my own. . . ."

"But you'll want a courting buggy when you are sixteen . . ." began Shoo-Fly.

"Bill's gonna buy a secondhand car and let me ride in it." Jonas turned the radio a little higher.

"*Ach, don't!*" cried Shoo-Fly. "Dat will hear it. The radio is a sin!"

"Bill says it's not a sin for him, so I say it's not a sin for me."

Shoo-Fly looked at him with eyes as big as his own conscience.

"But Bill's not Amish, and you are," she said.

"Not unless I join the Amish church, I'm not," said Jonas.

That night the Fishers had a visitor.

Shortly after Dat came back from town, a large black car drove into the barnyard and a big heavy man got out. Dat had met him at the Horse Sale in New Holland and told him to come. He took him to the stable and showed him his own horses. They talked about horses for a long time. Dat said he would like to raise five or six colts just to watch them grow and to break them to harness. The man wanted to buy a good riding horse and asked Dat to help him select one.

"What do you want with a horse?" asked Dat, laughing. "You've got a Cadillac!"

"After a day at the Lancaster stock market," the man said, "I want to come out here and ride and forget all my business troubles. I like this beautiful farm country. I want to go horse-back riding on these back roads."

"So that's it!" Dat laughed again. "A good horse you must have then. We'd like you to stay and eat with us."

"You mean I can?" asked the man. "I thought you plain people didn't mix with outsiders."

"Sometimes we do," said Dat, smiling.

The man went to his car and brought out some packages.

As soon as he came in the back door, Shoo-Fly recognized him. It was the Mystery Man from Massachusetts. She ran into the back bedroom. She did not want to see him. She had not forgotten that he had nearly crashed into her with his big car. She hated him. But she had to come out of hiding when supper was ready.

"Hi, there, Shoo-Fly Girl!" the man said. "How's the pie business today?"

Shoo-Fly hung her head and did not answer.

"I almost ran over you, didn't I?" The man laughed.

But Shoo-Fly did not think it was funny.

The naphtha gas lamp made a bright glow over the long table. The twins went dancing up and down on the long benches, put-ting silver and dishes in place. Hayfork and Sammy picked up knives and forks, hooked them together for make-believe airplanes, and zoomed them through the air. The man sat in the tulip rocker and watched. He did not say much.

Once he turned to Mam and said, "I like the plain people. I like the way your children *work*. My kids never did a lick of work in their lives."

Supper was plain but good. Home-canned sausage, carrots, potatoes, applesauce, chow-chow and canned peaches. The children crept out of the shadows and sat in their places. They prayed in silence. The man prayed and ate with them quietly, not talking. Shoo-Fly kept her eyes on her plate. She did not look at him once.

After the meal, he helped with the dishes. Then he opened his packages. He had gifts of dolls and toys, coloring books and crayons. There were pretty handkerchiefs for the older girls and penknives for Jonas and Rags. He offered a doll to Shoo-Fly, but she did not take it. He did not know she was too old to play with dolls. She went back in a dark corner and sat down.

The man leaned back in his rocker and talked about himself, as Dat asked him questions. He told about his business and his wealth. He said he had to come to Lancaster twice a year on business. He said his sons were in college and had cars of their own. He said he gave his daughter a beautiful home with all modern conveniences for a wedding present. He told about his wife and all her social activities and how many clubs she belonged to. He said he had so much money he didn't know what to do with it . . . so he thought he'd buy a good riding horse!

Jonas sat on the edge of his chair and listened to the man's words. He was absorbing a vision of an unknown world. Shoo-Fly watched him anxiously. She wished the man would stop talking and go home. He was giving Jonas too many ideas.

Then he did go. Dat promised to help him select a good riding horse. Dat and Jonas walked out to his car with him. When they came back, Jonas whispered to Shoo-Fly, "I wish I had a big Cadillac like that!"

Shoo-Fly ran to Dat. "Don't sell him Sonny Boy. He's a Grossmama horse. Grossmama needs him. She paid two hundred dollars for him."

Dat laughed. "Don't worry. He doesn't want an old plug like that!"

"Why does he come here to see us?" asked Shoo-Fly.

"He likes the plain people," said Dat.

CHAPTER VI

City of Strangers

Shoo-Fly was very excited. She could hardly stand still while Bib combed her hair. Today she was going to town. She had thought about it for a long time, and now at last the day had come. Shoo-Fly had to have new shoes and Rags a new felt hat. So they were going to New Holland. Mam said the twins could go too.

Shoo-Fly had her own money in her little purse. She knew just

97

what she was going to buy. She had a secret all her own.

Jonas hitched up Skipper to the buggy.

"What an old *cheese crate!*" said Jonas. "I hope it will hold together till you get home again."

Shoo-Fly laughed. "This is Grossmama's buggy. Where's Mam's?"

"It's at the shop for repairs," said Jonas. "One wheel squeaks. Besides, if a cheese crate's good enough for Grossmama, it's good enough for the family!"

The twins sat up front with Mam and Dat. Shoo-Fly and Rags sat in the back, with the curtain rolled up. It was Shoo-Fly's favorite place. She loved to watch the road flowing endlessly away out from under her. It was as if the buggy were standing still and the road itself were moving away. She knew the landscape for a mile or two, every tree and bush and fence. It was her own road, where every bird and butterfly, every horse and cow was a friend. Even the clouds in the sky were familiar, a part of her very life.

The road dipped into a valley past Uncle John's house, past the Zooks' farm, then over the old covered bridge, past fields of corn and alfalfa and woodland, then up the hill again, then took a turn after a pause at the junction. After that, the sharp noise of the horse's hoofs on the cement told her they were on the highway.

"There's where the pie stand used to be," she said, pointing.

Shoo-Fly was glad it was gone now. The weather had turned cooler, and there was little sale for baked goods. She had not gone back again after the near crash from the Mystery Man's car.

From here on, the highway was strange. From here on, she

was in a new world. New scenery opened up, with odd and unfamiliar homes and trees and yards, a few scattered shops and gas stations, and everywhere signs to read—in English. This went on and on, and suddenly they were in the city, with houses and shops all close together. Dat knew just where to go to tie up Skipper at a tie rack in the shade, in a parking lot behind a big store. They came around to the front. Here Dat left them, and Mam and the children walked slowly along the street.

"We'll just look first," said Mam.

The new world of the city was very exciting.

They went in and out of the stores. They stood outside looking in first one shopwindow, then another. It was wonderful just to look, look, look at all the lovely things. Dolls and toys and books and magazines, and dresses—stylish, fancy dresses of bright and colorful patterns, the kind the "English" people wore. They looked without envy, without any longing for the things they saw.

They came back to the large store and went in. Mam led the way through the crowded aisle. They found a stairway and went down to the basement. Here there were long tables and shelves filled with rolls of cloth on display. Shoo-Fly and her sisters walked up and down the aisles, touching the shiny silks and woolly fabrics. They rubbed their fingers on smooth satin and soft velvet. It took Mam a long time to pick out what she wanted. She bought material for shirts, pants, dresses and aprons.

Upstairs at the front counter, Reuben had to be fitted for a new hat. A stack of men's and boys' Amish hats was piled on the counter. The man clerk looked till he found one the right size. He tried to joke with Reuben, but the boy kept his mouth closed tight. He did not even smile. Was he afraid of the big city? Too?

They came to the shoe department and sat down. A lady clerk seemed to know just the right kind of shoe, and the right size for Shoo-Fly. They were black shoes with laces, and had patent-leather toes. They did not pinch at all, so Mam bought them.

Out on the street again, they walked several blocks and came to the Dutch Gift Shop. As they opened the door, a bell tinkled and a clerk came forward. It was Aunt Suzanna in her Amish dress, with her prayer covering on her head. She smiled and in her quiet way made them welcome.

The shop was filled with beautiful gifts. Shoo-Fly had never been there before. It was like a visit to dreamland. She looked and looked but could not see everything. Shelves and counters were filled with glass, china and knickknacks. The children looked but did not touch. Mam and Aunt Suzanna talked. The owner of the shop came and talked too.

Then Aunt Suzanna gave each of the children a present. She gave Rags a china pig bank, the twins tiny Amish dolls, and Suzanna a pink glass bonbon dish. Shoo-Fly thought it was the most beautiful thing in the shop.

"This will be for your hope chest," said Aunt Suzanna.

She packed the dish carefully in a cardboard box, and set it aside. Shoo-Fly said, "Thank you very much."

Then she remembered her secret. She whispered to Aunt Suzanna and Aunt Suzanna told her what to do. While the others went in the back room to visit, Shoo-Fly walked down the street alone.

She must remember the directions. Go to the corner, pass two green lights and cross over. The third store on the right was the Variety Store. There she could make her purchase. Shoo-Fly marched along, feeling very grown up. She looked neither to right nor left. She counted the lights, crossed over and found the store. She went in and looked around. She had never bought anything alone before. Her heart began to pound. The counters were filled with all sorts of things—notions and toys, stationery, soaps and jewelry.

Suddenly somebody called, "Hello! Why, it's Suzanna!"

She looked up. There were the Fergusons, Mrs. Ferguson, Betty, Janice and Bobby. It was good to see them. After all, they were neighbors.

"What are you doing in New Holland?" Betty asked.

"I came with my mother," said Shoo-Fly.

Betty was looking at barrettes. Her hair was *strubbly,* it hung all over her face. She needed something to hold it back.

"Buy me this one!" "I want that one!" Betty and Janice pointed to things they wanted. Bobby wanted candy and toys. Their mother bought them what they asked for.

Shoo-Fly watched in amazement. How greedy Betty was! She wanted everything she saw. Some Amish girls had bobby pins and a few wore very plain barrettes. But Mam said they were not necessary. A narrow black ribbon would keep the hair knot in place. The plain people did not wear fancy things. The first thing an Amish child learned was to deny himself.

The Fergusons left the store and Shoo-Fly found the harmonicas. The clerk was kind. She showed her the different kinds. It was hard to choose. One was called "Echo," one "Marine Band," and one "De Luxe Chromatic." She decided on a "Super 40 Chromatic" complete with leather case.

"Can you play, honey?" asked the clerk.

Shoo-Fly shook her head. "It's not for me," she said.

"All the Amish boys like them," said the clerk.

Shoo-Fly nodded. How well she knew it. They all loved music, and the harmonica was the only musical instrument allowed by

the Bishop. The big Amish boys bought very expensive ones, up to fifteen dollars, to play at their Sunday night "sings." She had heard Uncle Chris tell about it.

She paid her money and took her package. How glad she was now that she had saved her money. If only she could play it herself! Maybe she would try. She'd like to play her favorite songs, "Oh, Susanna!" and "Old McDonald Had a Farm."

She walked happily along the street. How surprised Jonas would be! Now he could give the borrowed radio back to Bill Ferguson before he got into trouble about it. He could forget the idea of going to Canada with Bill. He could stay at home and be happy with his new harmonica. And pretty soon when he got to be sixteen, Dat would buy him a fine riding horse and build him a shiny new buggy, and he could go visit a girl friend and start growing a beard. . . .

Suddenly Shoo-Fly looked around and wondered where she was. Everything looked strange. She stopped. She had never been here before. Had she started in the wrong direction? Where was she? The Variety Store was not in sight. And where was Aunt Susanna's gift shop? Which way had she come? And how could she cross the street where there was no traffic light?

Everywhere she looked, she saw words. English words jumped out at her from signs, posts, shop fronts and advertisements. *Cafeteria, Restaurant, Garage, Market, Insurance, Krafts, Colgate, Beauty Salon, Investment, Credit, Bumper Sale, Florist, Appliances.* She could read them all, but they did not help her. They only confused her. Where was the gift shop and what was its name? Had she ever heard it? She could not remember.

A cold wind began to blow. A black cloud loomed overhead. Shoo-Fly hugged her shawl closer. She clutched her purse and package tightly. She was hungry now. It was long past mealtime and she had not eaten since morning. Mam had promised them a treat—ice cream cones. But oh, it was too cold.

She walked along, not knowing where to go. She knew now she was lost. Where should she go? Which way should she turn? Sick at heart, she kept on going. Noises pounded on her ears, bells clanging, traffic drumming, whistles blowing, a siren wailing, a jukebox throbbing, all bringing confusion. For the first time she had come face to face with a remote and unfamiliar world.

Could she ask somebody? Whom could she ask? How could she talk to these strangers who passed her by? Strange people, "English" people, talking English, nothing but English. Men without beards, women with short skirts and pink legs showing to their knees, hair cut off part way and hanging loose as if they had just climbed out of bed. Women with spike heels to make them trip and fall. Strange creatures from another world. Worldly people, with worldly ways . . . greedy people who wanted everything they saw . . . little girls asking for everything in the store . . .

Shoo-Fly kept on going blindly. Maybe she would see a kind Amish person to ask. . . . She tried to keep the tears back.

Then somebody called, and there were the Fergusons again.

"Are you looking for somebody, Suzanna?" asked Mrs. Ferguson. "How did you get to town?"

"I came with my mother," said Shoo-Fly.

"You drove all the way in your buggy?" asked Mrs. Ferguson. Shoo-Fly nodded.

"Where is your mother now?" asked Mrs. Ferguson.

"At Aunt Suzanna's gift shop," said Shoo-Fly.

"Could we take you . . ." Mrs. Ferguson began.

"Oh, no! No, no, thank you!" said Shoo-Fly quickly.

She might be lost, but she could not ride in the Fergusons' car again. She had promised Mam not to do it.

She said good-by politely and hurried on. She was still lost. She might have asked where the gift shop was, but she didn't. She must look for an Amish woman. . . .

She saw Amish buggies go by but they did not stop. They all seemed to be going in the same direction. She turned several corners and came to a large hitching lot. Beside it was a big building with halls and stairs and passageways. Many people were going in and out, Amish people and others too. She could hear pigs squealing and cows mooing. Then she heard horses neighing. She knew now. It was the Stock Sales Barn, the place where farm animals were bought and sold.

This was the place where the Mystery Man was going to buy a riding horse. Was he here today? And would he know her if he saw her again? Maybe Dat was in there with him now, and they'd soon come out, and he would be riding a fine new horse!

Shoo-Fly saw Amish men with beards and black felt hats go in and come out, but no women at all. No Amish woman to help her. She hugged her shawl closer. She turned back and tried to remember the way she had come. She must get back to Main Street again. She turned a corner and came to a wider street. Was this the street where all the stores were?

She looked across. There was an Amish woman—it looked like Katie Zook's mother! Mrs. Zook would help her! Oh, she must catch her ... quick ... She darted out. *I mustn't let her get away ... I can run ...*

"STOP!"

Cry of brakes, a horrible screech ... someone shouts ...

The cars came to a halt. Shoo-Fly found herself in the middle of the street. Terrified, she turned and ran again. The cars started on. Safe on the other sidewalk at last, but Mrs. Zook was gone.

All at once everything was too much for her, the noise, the confusion, the strangeness, the queer people, the crowded stores and all the cars swooping by. She stopped, and the tears came. She leaned against a tree and cried as if her heart would break. How would she ever get home again ... ?

Back at the gift shop, Mam and the children waited. Why did not Shoo-Fly come? What was keeping her so long?

Aunt Suzanna grew nervous and flustered.

"I should never have let her go alone. But I thought she was old enough. .... All she had to do was to pass two traffic lights and cross over."

"Where was she going?" asked Mam.

"It is a secret." Aunt Suzanna smiled. "I don't like to tell."

"But we've had our sandwiches and she'll be hungry," said Mam.

"She said she'd come right back in time to eat." Aunt Suzanna wrung her hands. *"Ach,* now, why didn't I go with her?"

They sat down and talked again. But Shoo-Fly did not come. Then Mam grew restless.

"Maybe she found someone she knew . . ." began Aunt Suzanna. "Maybe she found Rufus and went to the Cow Sale." But she knew she was only guessing.

Mam could wait no longer. She picked up her bundles and they hurried down the street. They asked people, strangers, "English" people, if they had seen a lost Amish girl. They asked at stores and restaurants and houses. But no one had seen her. They met the Fergusons. Yes, they had seen and talked to her twice, but did not remember which way she went. They looked in the department store, but the clerks had not seen her.

By this time Reuben's face looked white and worried. The twins began to cry. Mam hurried faster than ever. They could hardly keep up.

Then at last, right on the corner by the store, Mam saw Dat and told him the story. He had been at the Cow Sale, but had not seen Shoo-Fly either. He stroked his beard and grew thoughtful. He told Mam to calm herself.

"We'll find her," he said. "A big girl like Suzanna would not get lost."

His words were quiet and patient. He even smiled.

"A wise little girl like our Suzanna cannot disappear in thin air!" he said. The children giggled. "Let's go get in the buggy."

"*Ach,* now, you're not even going to *hunt* for her?" began Mam, still sick with worry. "We'll have to go to the police station."

"I want to find Shoo-Fly . . ." wailed Punkin.

"Let's look for Susie . . ." wept Puddin.

Only Reuben, Rags, said nothing. His lips were fixed in a thin straight line. His eyes showed the sadness he felt. They all knew now how much they loved their sister.

"First," said Dat, "let's all have a treat. Who wants an ice cream cone?"

The children brightened. "I do!" "I do!" said the twins.

"Let's look for Shoo-Fly," said Rags.

"Ice cream comes first," said Dat. "We can't miss our treat."

Even Mam thought he was being foolish and wasting time. But they went in the drugstore, and she waited patiently while they nibbled and licked their cones.

"Now we'll go get in the buggy," said Dat.

"In the buggy?" cried Mam. Her patience had come to an end. "You're going to drive home and leave one of your children behind in this big city? Rufus, I can't understand you!"

Dat shooed the children before him.

"In the buggy—we'll find her!"

He never spoke truer words.

Skipper whinnied, he was so glad to see them and eager to get started for home.

Rags jumped up first, and started to step over the front seat. Then he jumped back, crying out in a loud voice, *"I found her! Here she is!"*

They could hardly believe it. There was Shoo-Fly in the back of the buggy. She had been curled up, fast asleep. She rubbed her eyes, trying to remember.

Everybody asked her questions at once, and all the way home she had to tell and retell her story.

She told how she had gone to the Sales Barn but had not found Dat at all. Somehow from there she had found her way back to Main Street and there by a traffic light she had located the big department store. She knew this was the place where Mam had bought her new shoes and Reuben's new hat. From there she had gone to the parking lot behind and found Skipper and the buggy.

She had climbed in the buggy—it was a perfect hidey-hole, a place to rest and be safe. She knew the others would come and find her there. She curled up on the blanket in the back and soon fell fast asleep.

"Wise girl!" said Dat. "It was the best thing for you to do."

"I knew you couldn't go home without me," said Shoo-Fly. Then she remembered. "I'm hungry," she said. "I haven't had a bite to eat since breakfast."

"*We* had ice cream cones," said Punkin and Puddin.

Mam pulled out a big bag of pretzels and opened it. The children nibbled all the way home.

Oh, how good it was to be home again, to see the big double house and the big bank barn, the spring house and tall, squeaking windmill still the same but different. The four martin houses, empty now, standing like sentinels along the fence. All so familiar, yet now more beloved, seen with new eyes after a long day's absence. The place so neat, so tidy, nothing to mar the simple beauty. The place so plain where so much exciting living went on, the place so plain called home.

Home was a shelter from the world and all things worldly.

The World Turns Upside Down

CHAPTER VII

The Gift Rejected

"*Ouch! Ouch!* Stop pulling!" cried Shoo-Fly. "You don't need to pull my hair out by the roots! Now, I'll do the rest myself."

Beck went away and left her.

Shoo-Fly was in a hurry. She seemed always to be in a hurry. She was never still a minute. Now she wanted to do two things —to see Jonas and to go over to Grossmama's.

112

She could comb her own hair! She'd show Beck she could do it herself. She parted her hair down the back. She made a tight twist over each ear, then coiled the long hair into two coils in the back and rolled them in a knot. She fastened it with hairpins. She looked in the mirror over the sink. It looked fine.

Mam came and said, "Good. You can do it yourself from now on. No more braids—you're not a little girl any longer. You must learn to sew too."

"*Ach,* but Mam, I want to . . ."

"You can use the sewing machine today," said Mam. "You can't learn any younger."

Shoo-Fly sat down at the sewing machine. Sewing was hard work. She had to guide the cloth, turn the wheel with her hand and press the treadle with her feet—everything at once. It was not easy to do.

Mam had cut out Shoo-Fly's new Sunday dress. It was a deep rich blue-green, a real Amish "peacock," her favorite color. Mam allowed a deep hem in the skirt and she put tucks in the upper part of the long sleeves, because Shoo-Fly was growing so fast. The dress had to last a long time. Shoo-Fly was sewing up the seams.

It was to be a grown-up dress, Shoo-Fly's first.

It would not button in the back like a little girl's dress. It would be pinned in front. It would have a *lepli,* a flat loose rounded flap in the back, with pleats in the skirt beneath. She would get a black cape to wear on her shoulders to match her black apron. And a new black bonnet, too—Mam was making it for her. All this meant she was no longer a little girl.

It was worth a lot of jabs from the needle and broken threads and rethreading, just to get a new outfit like this.

"*Wow!*" cried Shoo-Fly. "I almost sewed my finger again!"

"Try to be more careful," said Mam.

"You press the treadle too hard," said Beck. "Take it easy. Don't be in such a hurry."

But she *was* in a hurry. She wanted to get out and see Jonas. And she wanted to go over to Grossmama's. Why did she have to stay in and sew?

Beck was sewing too. Mam had two sewing machines, one for herself and the other for the girls to learn on. Shoo-Fly knew that the Zooks had four machines because they had eight girls. Mam was saving her egg money to get a third machine. Not an electric, of course, for the Amish do not have electricity. But Mam said she needed an automatic, the kind that would make buttonholes and fancy stitches and sewed backwards.

Bib was doing the cooking and housework so Mam could sew. The Amish buy no ready-made clothes, so there was plenty of sewing to do for Dat and the boys, and for the five girls and herself. All the girls were to get new Sunday dresses, so they could take their old ones for school. The boys were to get new suits. So the sewing room was a busy place.

Hayfork and Sammy crawled about on the floor. They were playing *bears* and chasing each other. They crawled in under Shoo-Fly's sewing machine and out again. She kicked them each time they went through. They went out the door onto the porch,

dragging things behind them.   Shoo-Fly heard them teasing the
pet crow outside.

"Hand me the scissors," said Beck.

"Scissors?   I haven't had the scissors," said Shoo-Fly.

"Where are they then?"

The scissors were gone and no one could find them.

Shoo-Fly heard the crow cawing outside.   Jackie was calling
her to come.   First she would go to Grossmama's because Great-
Grossmama was there.   She wanted to show them her new glass
dish.   Then she would hunt up Jonas.

She had been trying to see Jonas ever since her trip to town.
She wanted to see him alone, to give him the harmonica.   But
whenever she saw him, he was always off in a rush.   He came in
the house to eat, then rushed out and away.   He did not tease her
or call her pet names any more.

If she could only see him alone . . . Shoo-Fly got up from her
chair.

"Don't you run away now," said Beck.   "Just look at all the
snipples on the floor to clean up.   Go get the broom and dust
pan."

Shoo-Fly gave the floor a lick and a promise.   Then she went
flying out the door.   Jackie flew down to her shoulder.   He must
be hungry.   She ran to the barn and got him a handful of grain.
She must feed him to keep him from flying off for good.   She
slipped up to her room through the kitchen and brought down
the box with her new glass dish.

Great-Grossmama had come for a visit at Grossmama's.   She

was alert and active at ninety-one, and still had a home of her own. But she enjoyed visiting her children.

Shoo-Fly hurried over to Grossmama's house. She opened the door and looked in. The twins were not there. The coast was clear.

"Hello, Great-Grossmommy! How are you?" called Shoo-Fly.

Great-Grossmama sat in the tulip rocker, working on a braided rug. She sewed without glasses. Her fingers were never idle. She looked very tiny, sitting in the big old-fashioned rocker. But her eyes were bright and shining in her wrinkled face. She took Shoo-Fly's hand and kissed her.

"*Ach* now, what a big girl you are! Too heavy for me to hold. Soon a young lady you will be, that's for sure."

Shoo-Fly told her that she could now comb her own hair and that her new bonnet was to be *black*. And her new dress was to have a *lepli* in back and be pinned in front.

"Just like a *woman!*" Great-Grossmama cackled with laughter. "Then there is one thing more you need."

She reached into her sewing basket and picked up a bright-colored pincushion and gave it to Shoo-Fly.

"For your pins!" she said. "I will make another one to match. You must have a pair—just for fancy!"

"Oh, thank you, Great-Grossmommy!" said Shoo-Fly.

The pincushion had a star design cross-stitched in wool in bright blue and gay cerise. It had a ruffled lace border edge. It was beautiful.

"A girl must always be careful with pins," said Great-Grossmama. "Do not drop one. When you see a pin, pick it up. A girl needs many pins, at least fifteen, to dress properly. Five for your dress, five for your apron and five for your cape."

"*Ach,* but Great-Grossmommy . . ." Shoo-Fly hesitated. Should she speak or not? "Why do we have to *pin* our dresses? Why can't we use buttons like other people?"

"*Ach* now, you an Amish girl and don't know that?" said Great-Grossmama. "A *little* girl can have buttons on the back of her dress, where she cannot see them. But when she grows up, she has pins in front. Why? To keep humble, to avoid false pride. We are the plain people. We eat plain, we live plain, we dress plain, to show that our hearts are not set on the things of this world, but above. We are Amish. These things we have

always done. So we will always do." She turned to her work. "I will finish this rug and give it to you. It will be for your bedroom, something to remember me by."

There was a hush in the room.

"Thank you, Great-Grossmama," said the girl in a low voice.

After a while she opened her box. She brought out the pink glass dish and said it was a present from Aunt Suzanna. She held the dish up to the light. It shone like the setting sun. It had a wavy ruffled openwork edge as if it were made of lace.

Great-Grossmama admired it. "Keep it carefully," she said. "You will soon be starting a marriage chest. There you will keep things for the home you will have someday. You are growing fast—it won't be long now." She leaned back in her rocker, closed her eyes and dozed off. The conversation had tired her.

Then Grossmama called her. "Come and help me, Susie."

Grossmama was making *schnitz*. Mam always said drying apples was Grossmama's job. Shoo-Fly could not escape. Grossmama put a paring knife in her hand, and before she knew it, she was busy peeling and cutting apples. Grossmama sat beside her, working too. Each apple had to be cut into *schnitz* or eighths.

"Do we have to do the *whole* bushel?" asked Shoo-Fly.

"Well, yes," said Grossmama, "and that won't be half enough for all the *schnitz* pies we'll want in the wintertime. I'll make a big wood fire in the oven in the kettle house and fill it up with all my trays of *schnitz* and put them in to dry. Plenty *schnitz* we must have for the winter."

They talked softly so they would not disturb Great-Grossmama.   Shoo-Fly peeled steadily until her hand began to get tired.

"All my meadow teas are dried already," Grossmama went on. "Peppermint, spearmint, sage, alfalfa.   Soon the attic will be full. What would we do without our teas? Alfalfa for arthritis, catnip tea for crying babies, and boneset for colds.   I kept all my children well and strong with meadow teas.   Who needs to run to the drugstore? No, no, the old remedies are best."

Shoo-Fly was tired of peeling.   It would soon be time for Aunt Suzanna to come home from work.   She glanced at the clock.   It was time for supper, and she hadn't seen Jonas yet.

"I've got to go now," she said.   "I've got to go set the table."

This time Grossmama made no objections.

Shoo-Fly picked up her box and went out.   She took the box up to her bedroom and hid it under her bed.   She put the new harmonica in the pocket under her apron and ran downstairs.

Bib was cooking supper.   The twins were out of sight and the little boys were building with blocks on the kitchen floor.

Bib called, "Did you take Mam's scissors? Mam wants you to look for her scissors.   She can't find them."

But Shoo-Fly was already outside.   Mam and Beck and Rags had gone out to milk.   The coast was clear.   Where was Jonas?

He must still be at the carriage shop.   She ran out the lane as fast as she could go.   Yes, the door was still open and she heard pounding on metal.   Was Dat still there working? Didn't he know it was time to stop and go help with the milking?

She crept in quietly.   She heard a murmur of voices.   It didn't

sound like Dat's hearty voice at all. Nor like Uncle Chris, who
always shouted. The voices were low and quiet and the pounding was a soft thudding. What was going on? She slipped in
past the broken-down buggies, past the extra wheels and shafts
and new tops and seats. The door to the forge room at the back
was partly open. She peeped in.

There he was—Jonas, at last!

Dat was not there. He must have gone back to help with the
milking, after all. Someone was with Jonas and it was not Dat.
It was Bill Ferguson. He and Jonas were pounding something
at the forge. They were talking in low voices.

Ach, it was terrible! He shouldn't be seeing Bill Ferguson all
the time. They must be planning to run away. Shoo-Fly did not
make a sound. But suddenly Jonas looked up and saw her.
Anger, like a black cloud, moved across his face and flashed in
his dark eyes.

"Get out!" he yelled. *"You get out of here!"*

Bill Ferguson jumped guiltily. Shoo-Fly turned and ran,
bumping into wheels and axles as she went.

"What are you always tagging after me for?" shouted Jonas.
"Why can't you leave me alone for a minute?"

Shoo-Fly left the carriage shop in a hurry. Jonas had often
teased her, and sometimes been angry with her. But not like
this, never before like this. She shook with fear. What had she
done? Why was he so angry? She started back down the lane,
then returned. She went to the corner of the carriage shop and
waited.

Whatever the boys were doing, they stopped. She heard Bill Ferguson say he had to go. They came out of the shop and Jonas closed the outside doors.

"Next week, then!" he called to Bill, who went off down the road. Then Jonas started on a run for home. He passed by Shoo-Fly without seeing her.

She tried to catch up. "Jonas! Jonas!" she called. "Wait for me. Wait for me, Jonas! I've got something for you ... Jonas ..."

Jonas heard her and stopped dead in his tracks. He waited till she came up.

"Jonas ... Jonas ..." Shoo-Fly began, breathless, "I've got something for you ... I want to give you ..." She reached in her secret pocket and touched the new harmonica in its leather case. The feel of it in her hand gave her courage.

"Suzanna, will you please *let me alone?*" shouted Jonas. His voice was changing and sounded hoarse. "I don't want to have anything to do with you! Please stop pestering me!"

"But you said you were going to ..." She wanted to say *run away,* but she couldn't. "I saved up my money and I bought you ..."

He was listening now. Maybe he wasn't so mad, after all. She pulled the harmonica out of her pocket.

"... a beautiful harmonica. ..." She handed it out, but he could hardly see it in the gathering darkness. "It's a *Super 40 Chromatic,*" Shoo-Fly said with pride. "The best kind they had in the store."

"A *harmonica!*" cried Jonas. "Can you beat that? *You* went and bought *me* a harmonica?" He could not believe it.

"*Ach, ja!*" said Shoo-Fly quietly. *Please God, make him like it,* she prayed. She wanted to tell him she had paid all her money for it, but she couldn't.

"A *harmonica! Jeepers!*" cried Jonas, roaring with laughter. "My kid sister buys me a harmonica! *Harmonica! Harmonica!*" He threw back his head and roared.

Shoo-Fly let it fall to the ground. She went suddenly limp and thought she was going to faint. Jonas didn't want it, after all. She couldn't cry, the hurt was too deep. She reached down, picked the hated object up from the ground and put it back in her pocket. He didn't want it, after all. All Amish boys liked harmonicas, but Jonas didn't want it.

"Oh, Jonas," she managed to say, "I don't want you to . . . run away. . . ."

The words made him angry again.

"*Run away?* Who said I'm going to *run away?*" he blustered. "Young lady, just don't you start making up things about me and getting me in trouble. . . ." He leaned over and shook his finger in her face. "What I do is *none of your business!* Understand?"

"Yes, Jonas," said Shoo-Fly in a whisper.

He ran on ahead of her, back toward the barn.

Shoo-Fly walked slowly. She could not think. She could not feel. Her world had turned upside down.

When she was halfway home, she stopped. She ran swiftly across the field.

She took the new harmonica out of her pocket and looked at it. She took it out of its case. She threw it as hard as she could toward the creek. She thought she heard it splash in the water. She threw the case after it. She never wanted to see it again. The trees were bare now and a cold wind was blowing. Winter would soon be here.

Then she walked home, and the world was all anger and pain and disappointment and sadness.

The next morning Uncle Chris put his head in at the back door. They were just finishing breakfast.

"The corn is ready for husking," he said. "The ears are falling over. That means it needs husking. We want to get it in before snow flies. Let's beat Uncle Dave. Am I going to have any helpers?"

"Me! Me! Me!" cried the children. The little boys ran and climbed all over Uncle Chris.

"After school, then," he shouted. "Don't forget."

So cornhusking began.

Every day after school, they all put on their oldest but warmest clothes and hurried out to the field. Dat closed his carriage shop and came, too. He did not want to miss the fun.

Cornhusking was a sort of winter picnic. It was always a family affair.

Shoo-Fly went along, just one in the big crowd. She did not want to be alone now, she did not want to see Jonas or talk to him. He never looked at her any more. It was a comfort to be surrounded by all the family, to hear them jabbering and teasing and frolicking. She wanted to forget her own thoughts. Nobody noticed how sad and quiet she was or how often she came near to tears.

Dat, Beck, Bib, Mam and Aunt Emma each took a row of their own. Reuben and Punkin took a row together, and Shoo-Fly and Puddin another. Jonas drove the wagon and they all picked and threw the ears over the sides. *Bang, bang, bang* went the corn hitting the empty wagon box. Uncle Chris came behind with the binder, cutting the corn, ready for putting it into shocks. Pretzel was there too, running everywhere and barking.

The older girls talked about school and lessons, and repeated things that other girls said. Mam and Aunt Emma talked about remedies for colds. A flock of pheasants roamed over the cut part of the field. The small boys ran to chase them. Crows flew overhead, cawing madly. Was Jackie with them? Shoo-Fly wondered. She fed him every day and he still liked to talk to her.

The first few days, it was fun out in the cornfield. Then the cold wind began to blow down from the north and it was hard to keep warm. In late afternoon, there was little or no heat from the sun, and many days were cloudy. The children lagged behind and could not be hurried.

"Come on now, let's sing!" cried Mam one day. "Each one his favorite song."

They all began to sing.

"Row, Row Your Boat," "Old Black Joe," "My Bonnie Lies over the Ocean," and "Polly Wolly Doodle" rang out over the field. The singing warmed cold bodies, but made the work go slower.

Shoo-Fly asked for "Oh, Susanna" and everybody laughed. But they sang it with gusto.

On the very last day, a dark cloud arose and the sky grew black. Then a misty dampness filled the air. Shoo-Fly's fingers began to freeze. . . . She could not work any more. She slumped behind, letting little Puddin get ahead. She did not care if they all got ahead. Her head ached and her throat felt sore.

"It's snowing!" cried Hayfork. "Look at the *snow!*" He began to dance a jig. "Wait till I make a snow man!"

The twins and the little boys began to cough and sneeze. Everybody was getting chilled. "Let's go home, now," wailed the little ones.

"*Ach* now," called Mam, "how about 'Jingle Bells' to pep us all up?"

They began to sing:

> *Jingle bells, jingle bells,*
> *Jingle all the way,*
> *Oh, what fun it is to ride*
> *In the one-horse open sleigh!*

Over and over they sang it, with all its verses, and it helped them get through to the very last row, and the very last ear of corn. That night a very tired family of children fell heavily into their beds, tired but happy that the winter frolic was over.

Shoo-Fly felt sick. She pulled the covers up but could not stop shivering.

CHAPTER VIII

Disaster Falls

Why was the bed so cold? Would she ever get warm again? Shoo-Fly opened her eyes and the dresses hanging on the wall were dancing. The bureau moved back and forth. Then Mam came in, not one Mam but two. How strange it was! Shoo-Fly tried to swallow the medicine but choked.

The twins were in bed too. And Rags and the two little boys. It was time for dinner. Why were all the children in bed? Everybody was coughing and sneezing, somebody was crying. Was

127

this a dream or was this the hospital?

Where were Beck and Bib? Why didn't they help Mam? They must be upstairs. Were they sick too? Mam stayed upstairs a long time. She did not come when Shoo-Fly called.

Jonas had a bad cough. Where was he now? Had he stopped coughing or gone away? Oh, that's right, Jonas ran away and it was all Shoo-Fly's fault. She must get up and stop him . . . how could she stop him . . . ?

"A car! A car! There's a man to buy eggs!"

The twins were shouting. Why couldn't they keep still? They had jumped out of bed, stepped over Shoo-Fly, run to the window and looked out. They rushed back to bed again. They kept on shouting.

"He's bringing a big box in the house," cried Punkin.

"He's bringing us a present," cried Puddin.

"Land sakes!" said Mam. "Why does he have to come now, when I have my hands so full?"

Shoo-Fly knew now. It must be the Mystery Man from Massachusetts. She never wanted to see him again. There he was at the back door, knocking. Mam let him in and he boomed a cheerful hello. He said he had not made up his mind about a horse yet, but he had brought a little present for his "sweethearts."

The twins jumped up and down on the bed. Shoo-Fly bounced up and down with them. They could hear the man talking.

"What's the matter?" he asked. "Is something wrong?"

"I'm running a hospital," said Mam. "All the children are sick in bed. We had to husk the corn and they all caught colds."

The man looked in the bedroom and waved at the twins. "I'm

not afraid of germs," he bragged. He hauled the big box into the kitchen and took the covering off.

The twins danced around on Shoo-Fly's bed. They jumped over the boys' bed, where sick Reuben, Hayfork and Sammy were sleeping. They could not wait any longer. They ran out into the kitchen in their nightgowns.

"Oh! The dollhouse!" cried Punkin.

"The dollhouse that Grossdawdy Yoder made!" Puddin clapped her hands.

The twins looked it over, then ran and found little dolls to put inside. They got little boxes and pieces of cloth. They started housekeeping.

"They're not very sick," said the man.

"No," said Mam. "Not like the others."

"But I thought it was for *your* little girls," said Punkin, sitting on the man's lap. He had one on each knee now.

"It *is* for *my* little girls," said the man. "Their names are Punkin and Puddin—they are my two little girls! But where is . . . where is that little Shoo-Fly Girl who bakes shoo-fly pies?"

"She's in *there*—we'll get her!"

The twins ran and dragged Suzanna out of bed. They pulled her into the kitchen. She was so dizzy she could hardly walk.

"Look what we've got!" they cried, pointing. "He brought it for us!"

Shoo-Fly looked. She remembered seeing the dollhouse at Grossdawdy Yoder's. She bent down and looked inside.

"How do you like it?" the man asked.

Shoo-Fly looked up. Her eyes looked like big black saucers

in her pale face.   "The stairs don't go nowhere . . ." she said.

"Haw, haw, haw!"   The Massachusetts man tipped his head back and roared.   "Can you beat that?   'The stairs don't go nowhere. . . .' "

Shoo-Fly slipped back into bed.

Let him laugh.   She didn't care.   She hated him anyhow.

The next day Mam told her she could get up.   The first thing she did when she went outside again was to call Jackie.   But the crow did not come.   Nobody had fed him while she was sick. Where was Jackie?   She called and called, but he did not come.

Then Mam said she was well enough to go to school, so she went.   It was good to see Miss Weber again.   And also Betty Ferguson.   Betty put her arm around her, and said Suzanna was her best friend.   Betty said she liked her better than all the other

girls in the school. The warmth of Betty's friendship was welcome to her starved heart.

At recess, Suzanna ran to the cupboard to get the bat and ball and gloves as usual. Outside she began to direct the ball game, as she had done so many times before. She got the boys and girls lined up to play. She was first batter. She hit the ball hard, then started running. But she did not get to first base. She ran zigzag, then turned suddenly, and ran back toward the school door.

"Susie!" screamed the others. "Where are you going?"

They were all angry with her, but she did not care.

She could not play ball today. She went inside and sat down in her seat. She folded her arms on her desk and bent her head down on them. She felt faint inside and began to cry. The tears came in a rush.

Miss Weber came over. "Are you all right, Suzanna?" she asked.

"Yes, Miss Weber," said Suzanna.

"Are you crying, Suzanna?"

"No, Miss Weber, doing my lessons." She tried to sniff the tears back. She took her hanky from her secret pocket and blew her nose.

"Are you sure you are well again, Suzanna?" asked Miss Weber.

"Yes, Miss Weber."

"Here are some good books you will like," said Miss Weber. "The bookmobile from Lancaster stopped while you were out sick, and I saved these for you. Look them over and take one home with you."

Suzanna thanked her. But when school closed, she left the books lying on her desk. She did not feel like reading. The boys dashed ahead on their scooters and the girls followed, walking slowly. They chattered and giggled, but Suzanna did not listen. Katie Zook began a long tale about the time her uncle took her to the Philadelphia Zoo and what all the animals looked like. She said it was all right for Amish people to look at wild animals because God made them. . . .

Suzanna lagged behind. She wished now she had brought the new library book after all. She would go to bed when she got home and read the book under the covers—if she could only find Jonas' flashlight. Why didn't she bring the book? Her head ached. . . . If only Katie Zook would stop talking . . .

The twins ran on ahead and turned in at the lane. They did not wait for her. The twins were always happy together. They did not need anyone else. They were always running off and leaving Suzanna alone.

Shoo-Fly walked home so slowly, the twins got there long before she did. As she walked through the barnyard, she called Jackie. She went in the barn and got some grain. She called and called but Jackie did not come. She threw the grain to the gabbling geese. Where was Jackie?

Shoo-Fly went indoors and took off her school clothes. She put on her old ones. She watched the twins playing with the new dollhouse. Mam was sewing and asked her to look for the lost scissors. Shoo-Fly came out again.

She called Jackie, but the crow did not come.

It was quiet in the barnyard, no noisy crows, no shouting children—even the geese were quiet. They did not know that their days were numbered, that they would be butchered, dressed and sold to be roasted, or that they would be canned for meat to be eaten on a cold winter day. The barnyard was so quiet, it was like the calm before a storm.

All at once, out of the silence came the sharp hoofbeats of a running horse. *Clop, clop, cloppety, clop,* a horse came tearing along the lane and direct into the barnyard. Could it be one of the aunts coming for a visit? No . . .

There came Sonny Boy, a wild look in his eye, with the long lines of his harness dangling. . . . Sonny Boy with his harness on . . . Where was the buggy? Sonny Boy, the nice old tame "Grossmama horse" . . . where was Grossmama's buggy, and *where was Grossmama?*

Shoo-Fly flew into the house.

"Mam! Mam! Look!" She pointed out the window. *"Sonny Boy!"*

"What? Where?" cried Mam. She was combing her hair. Out the window she saw the horse and knew that something had happened. The next minute her long hair was coiled and pinned in a knot. She ran out the door.

Shoo-Fly followed her. "I told Grossmama buggies are dangerous," but Mam did not hear.

Mam caught Sonny Boy by the bridle, patted him on the nose and talked to him to quiet him. She tied him to the tie rack by the fence.

The next minute a truck came bouncing into the barnyard. It came very fast and pulled up to a sudden stop. A man got out. It was Adolph Kinzer, the owner of the hardware store in town. He got out and said a few words to Mam. All Shoo-Fly heard was the word "accident."

Without a word, Mam got in the truck and rode away. Without a word to Shoo-Fly, she was gone. Mam went away without her bonnet, without even her prayer covering. Something terrible had happened. Shoo-Fly had never seen her mother outdoors without her covering. It was a shocking sight. Mam bareheaded! Going to town bareheaded!

What should she do? Shoo-Fly thought of Jonas first, then of her father. It did not take her long to run across the field. Dat was at the forge, heating a heavy piece of iron red-hot. Jonas was taking nails out of the tire rim of a wheel. The minute they saw her, they knew something was wrong.

"Grossmama's horse . . . Mam went away with Mr. Kinzer in

his truck . . ." It was hard to get the words out.

They left everything as it was. They ran to the barn and hitched up Skipper. Dat and Jonas jumped in the buggy and started off down the road.

Shoo-Fly went back in the house, filled with fear. The twins were crying and Hayfork and Sammy were fighting. Rags came in and she told him what had happened.

Rags wasted no time in worry or tears. Rags behaved like a little man. "We better do the chores," he said.

"But where are Bib and Becky? Why don't they come?" asked Shoo-Fly.

"Let's start the milking," said Rags. "You feed the cows and I'll get the milk pails."

"I'll help too," said Henry. "Give me that hayfork." They went to the barn and Hayfork was true to his nickname. He took the big hayfork and pitched hay like a man, while the others milked the cows.

Rags poured the milk into the cans and he fed the barn cats. The mother cat, Becky Green-Eyes, came, and all the others.

Out in the barnyard, Shoo-Fly called Jackie again. But the crow did not come. What had happened to Jackie? Jackie must be lost. Maybe he was in trouble somewhere. . . . But Shoo-Fly could not go looking for him now. The little children came running out crying. She went in the kitchen and made "cold soup" for them. She broke bread into little pieces and poured milk over it. She opened a can of peaches and poured them in.

How strange it was, without Dat and Mam! And without Jonas and the big girls. Why didn't they come home? Then she re-

membered. They were to go straight from school to Uncle Chris's
to help Aunt Emma with her *schnitzing*. They had planned to
stay all night. Without them, Shoo-Fly was the oldest girl and
had to be responsible. It was not easy, because all the time, fear
clutched at her heart, fear for her beloved little Grossmama.

The children dried their tears and sat down to eat. While they
ate, Shoo-Fly could hear the big clock ticking. She had never
noticed how loudly it ticked before. How long would they have
to wait for news of Grossmama?

It began to grow dark. "Can you light the lamp?" asked Rags.

"Not the gas lamp," said Shoo-Fly. "I'm afraid to pump it up.
It might explode."

Rags found a kerosene lamp and a match. He lighted the wick,
put the chimney back on and set it on the table. When it smoked,
he turned the wick down lower. The lamp threw a yellow glow
over the supper table. It lighted up the faces of the little ones.
It showed how dirty their faces were. Shoo-Fly had forgotten to
tell them to wash up before they ate. She forgot to tell them to
pray too. What would Mam say if she knew?

Shoo-Fly could not eat. Something had happened to Grossmama. Her horse had come home without her. Where was
Grossmama? And Dat and Mam? The poor old crow was gone
too. Shoo-Fly felt like crying, but held back her tears. If she
cried, the little ones would cry too. And she was ashamed to
worry about the crow when Grossmama was in trouble.

They waited a long time. They waited but nobody came.
Then Rags helped her put the children to bed.

The next morning, Shoo-Fly learned the worst.

Grossmama was in the hospital. She had been taken in an ambulance. They did not know how badly she was hurt. She had some broken ribs, and cuts and bruises. Aunt Suzanna was staying at the hospital with her.

The accident happened on the highway, no one knew just how. Evidently Grossmama had started to make a left turn, when a car came up unexpectedly. The car hit the buggy, knocking Grossmama out on the ground. The horse reared and plunged, tore loose and ran down the road. It had happened near the hardware store and Mr. Kinzer, an old friend of Grossmama's, had called the ambulance that took Grossmama to the hospital. He had taken Aunt Suzanna there, too. Dat and Mam went to the hospital, but found Grossmama too shaken up to talk. They were all thankful she was still alive.

Jonas brought the buggy home—what was left of it. Shoo-Fly went over to the carriage shop to see it. It was just a little pile of kindling wood. She started to ask Jonas about it. Then she saw that he had on his Sunday clothes. He was going somewhere.

"Where are you going, Jonas?" she asked. But he would not answer.

Now Grossmama's house was empty. It was cold, too, with the fires out. And dark in the evenings with no lamps lit. Shoo-Fly went in every day to water Grossmama's house plants. It made her sad to go in. She missed Grossmama badly.

Every day Dat went to see Grossmama at the hospital. One day when he came back, he shook his head. She was not making the progress she should.

"The doctor says it's her age. . . ."

"But she's only sixty-eight," said Mam.

"We'll both go tomorrow," said Dat. "I want you to see what you think."

Next day when they went, they took Beck and Bib with them. Mam left supper instructions for Shoo-Fly written on a paper: "Food is in pans on back of stove. Potatoes, gravy, beans. Warm it up."

It sounded easy. "I'll make a surprise," said Shoo-Fly.

She made the little ones stay in the bedroom until the meal was ready. She decided to make this a very special supper. It might help to make Grossmama well. She looked in the bottom drawer of Mam's bureau and got out her prettiest bedspread—the one with the big purple dahlias on it. She spread it on the table for a tablecloth.

She went over to Grossmama's house and up the dark, spooky back stairs to the still darker "good room." She had to feel around to find what she was looking for, two beautiful bay candles with flowers painted on them, standing in two pink glass candlesticks. They were Aunt Suzanna's. The gift shop lady had given them to her. Shoo-Fly knew that Aunt Suzanna wanted Grossmama to get well as much as anybody did. She would not mind having them used in a good cause.

Back in the kitchen, Shoo-Fly set the candlesticks in the center of the table and lighted them.

Supper was ready, so she went to the sideboard in the front room and brought out Mam's prettiest serving dishes. She served the warmed-up food in them. She put the bread on the best and biggest turkey platter. Now everything was ready.

She called the children in from the other room. Are your hands and faces clean? Yes! Yes! How surprised they were to see the kitchen looking so "fancy."

"Goody! Goody!" cried Punkin. "It's a party!" said Puddin.

At the back door she called and called Jonas and Rags to come. Rags came in without Jonas. Didn't he know it was time for supper? The food was getting cold. They sat down and folded their hands.

"But we can't pray till Jonas comes," said Shoo-Fly. "We're going to pray God to make Grossmama well."

They waited awhile, getting hungrier and hungrier. Then Jonas came banging in. He thumped down into Dat's place and growled, "What's going on here anyway?"

Shoo-Fly and the children dropped their eyes and prayed silently. Jonas had to pray, too. *Oh God,* prayed Shoo-Fly, *make Grossmama well and please make Jonas be nice to me again.* Then they began to eat.

Jonas reached for a potato with his fork, but he could not stick it in. He picked the potato up in his hand. It still had the skin on. He looked at it closely. He cut it with his knife.

"This potato is not cooked!" he cried. "It's *raw!* Who cooked this supper anyhow?"

"I did," said Shoo-Fly. "I did just what Mam said. She wrote it on a paper: 'Food is in pans. Warm it up.' That's what I did."

"Potatoes need boiling," said Jonas, disgusted. "Do you expect us to eat *raw food?*" Then he noticed the table. "What's this? What kind of a fancy tablecloth is this? And where did you get *candles?* What's going on here? Am I seeing straight or did I dream all this up?"

"*Ach,* Jonas, don't be mad . . ." begged Shoo-Fly.

"It's pretty," cried Punkin. "It's just for fancy!"

"We like it," said Puddin. "It's a sort of party to make Grossmama well."

"It don't do any harm," said Rags quietly.

Hayfork and Sammy began to tussle with each other.

Shoo-Fly tried to explain. "I thought we'd have a special supper and pray God to make Grossmama well and bring her home again . . ."

But Jonas was not listening.

"I've got all the milking to do . . ." He stalked out the back door.

What had happened to Jonas? He was like a different person.

He used to be a friend, but now Shoo-Fly could not understand him at all.

After he left, Shoo-Fly began to clear the table. She must get things put back before Mam returned. Even the twins began to be nervous. They kept running to the window to see if the horse and buggy had come in the barnyard. When Shoo-Fly folded up the quilt, she saw that Sammy had spilled a puddle of gravy on it. She tried to wash it off, but it left a bad stain. The quilt was a new one too. It had never been used before.

Rags went out to help with the milking and Hayfork to feed the cows. The twins helped wash dishes and put things away. The supper party was not much of a success, but at least they had prayed a good prayer for Grossmama. Even if Jonas didn't like it, Shoo-Fly hoped God was listening.

She went out to look for her crow. There beside the barn, she heard Jonas's radio going. He was playing it very loudly, as if he did not care who heard it. She held her ears—it was jazz!

Then the radio was turned off, the boys had come in and the little ones were safe in bed by the time Mam and Dat returned. The news was good—Grossmama was better. She was going to get well. Shoo-Fly smiled to herself. The prayer had helped.

But the days that followed were lonesome ones, with Grossmama's house empty and cold and dark.

And the pet crow gone. Every day Shoo-Fly called but he never came. Every day after school she looked for him. Whenever she saw a flock of crows, she called him by name.

She wanted her pet more than ever. She wanted to have something to love, that belonged to her alone. She searched the fields night after night. Maybe he had hurt a wing and could not fly. She would find him and bind up his wing, feed him and teach him to fly again. She asked everybody, but no one had seen the crow.

One afternoon she went over to the Fergusons'. Maybe they had seen the crow. Maybe Betty had fed it and it had stayed there. Shoo-Fly's hopes rose as she ran up to their door.

The room was bright with electric lights. The Fergusons were just getting up from their dining-room table. They were laughing and joking.

"You should have come sooner, Suzanna," said Mrs. Ferguson, "so you could have eaten with us."

"We had blackbird potpie for supper," said Betty. "Oh boy! Wasn't it delicious!"

"What?" asked Shoo-Fly. "What did you say?"

"Don't you know," said Betty, " 'four and twenty blackbirds baked in a pie'?"

" 'Blackbirds'?" asked Shoo-Fly.

Betty went on: " 'Down came a blackbird and pecked off her nose!' "

"But he didn't get it, did he?" cried Mr. Ferguson, laughing.

Betty put her hand over her nose. "No! Not this time."

Shoo-Fly was still puzzled. It was some "English" joke she did not understand. "I don't know what you are talking about," she said.

Betty explained. "A mean old blackbird was forever stealing Mommy's clothespins . . ."

Shoo-Fly's heart skipped a beat. She was right—the crow had been here.

"And dropping her nice clean washing down in the mud," Betty went on. She could hardly talk for laughing. "So when that mean old blackbird came down once too often on the clothesline . . . it was just too much . . . so Daddy shot it. . . ."

Shoo-Fly's face went white.

"And Mommy said it was probably tough, but she thought she could tenderize it in her pressure cooker. So she put it in a potpie and Daddy said we'd eat it . . . so we . . ."

Shoo-Fly turned away and Betty noticed something was wrong.

"Wait a minute," she said. "I was just joking! We didn't have blackbird pie at all. That was just a joke, Daddy's always joking. . . . It was *chicken* potpie really."

Shoo-Fly turned back. She might as well know the truth.

"But the bird . . . on the clothesline . . ." she began. "If it was

a chicken you killed, where . . . which way did the bird go when he flew away?"

"Oh!" cried Betty. "I told you. It didn't fly away. Daddy shot it . . . and buried it!"

Shoo-Fly turned quickly, but before she had gone two steps, she had to vomit.

Mrs. Ferguson came and caught her. "Why, honey, you're sick!" she cried. She tried to lead her to a couch to lie down, but Shoo-Fly broke away. She ran to the door. She could not get away fast enough.

At the door she stopped and looked back. Her eyes were big and dark in her thin little face. Her throat was sore and her head ached. But the hurt in her heart was worse than either of these.

"You killed my pet!" she said. "My pet crow Jackie! That's why I couldn't find him."

"Your pet?" cried Mr. Ferguson, astonished. "Did you have a pet crow? How could I know it was your pet? I didn't even know you had one."

"Betty knew it," said Shoo-Fly.

"But I didn't know it would ever come over *here*," said Betty.

"You knew it took clothespins away and let the clothes drop."

Betty hung her head. "I didn't think," she said.

Mr. Ferguson looked at Mrs. Ferguson and now he wasn't joking any more. "It was Suzanna's pet crow."

Betty ran to her father and cried out, "Daddy, you killed Suzanna's pet crow!" They all looked at each other in dismay.

But all their regret could not bring the crow back to the little girl who loved it so much.

The World Is Peace and Love

CHAPTER IX

Double Trouble

J ackie was dead. Shoo-Fly never knew how she got home from the Fergusons'. She walked unhappily through the barn-yard. Jackie was dead. The pet crow would no longer light on her shoulder again. She no longer had a pet to feed and care for. Jackie was dead.

She looked up and saw something strange. Skipper, Dat's driving horse, was hitched to the family buggy and tied to the rack. What did that mean? Was Dat going somewhere? Where would he be going at this time of the evening? The buggy had electric-battery lamps and they were lighted.

The kitchen door opened and Dat ... was it Dat? ... came out. No, it was not Dat. It was Jonas, and he was all dressed up in his Sunday clothes again. Why was he always dressing up?

"Where are you going?" Shoo-Fly asked.

Jonas walked past her without answering.

"Who told you you could take Dat's horse and buggy?" she asked.

Jonas walked quickly to the buggy, jumped in, slapped the lines and drove out the lane. He paid no attention to his little sister.

"Where are you going?" screamed Shoo-Fly.

But no answer came back.

Jonas was no longer a friend. Jonas would not talk to her any more. Did Dat say Jonas could take Skipper and go driving to town? A boy was supposed to wait till he was sixteen and get a horse of his own to drive, and not use the family horse. Was he going to that tavern where Bill Ferguson took him before? All her worries about Jonas flooded her mind.

Shoo-Fly rushed into the house, the dead crow forgotten now in this new crisis.

"Jonas is taking Skipper and going off somewhere!" she cried. *"Stop him! Stop him!"*

The children were crowded around Dat, who sat in the tulip rocker and held his big book on his lap. All the faces looked up at her in astonishment.

"Don't worry about Jonas," said Mam.   "Jonas is all right."

"Come and sit down, Susie," said Dat.   "Pull up a chair."

"But did you tell him he could take Skipper and the buggy?" cried Shoo-Fly, looking at Dat.   "He went driving off down the road lickety-split!"

"Yes," said Dat, quietly.   "I told you it's all right."

They did not care.   She could not tell them he was headed for Canada.   She had promised Jonas to keep it a secret.   She knew they would be sorry after he was gone.   They were helping him to go by letting him use the horse and buggy.   Dat and Mam did not know he was going to run away and become "English."   How could she warn them?

Shoo-Fly brought a low stool and sat down.   Her heart stopped pounding as she listened to Dat's quiet words.   Then she thought of the dead crow again, and the tears rolled down her cheeks.

"Don't you feel well, Susie?" asked Mam.

"I'm all right," said Shoo-Fly.   "I'm going to bed."

She could not tell anybody about the dead crow.   They would only laugh at her.   They had all hated the crow and wanted to see the last of him.   They would all be glad to know the mean old crow was gone.   She had to hold her sorrow in her heart and bury it there.   How could she ever be happy again?

Mam sent all the children to bed early.

"Get a good night's sleep," she said.   "We'll have a busy day tomorrow."

B-r-r-r! B-r-r-r!

The alarm clock kept ringing and ringing.   Shoo-Fly woke and lifted her head sleepily. She felt as if she had not slept at all. She reached over and shook the twins. It was time to get up. Beck and Bib were already dressed and going downstairs.

Today was Saturday. The family was going to strip tobacco. It was a long-drawn-out job that would last all winter. They would work all day on Saturdays, and before and after supper on school weekdays.

The big girls had breakfast ready at five-thirty, while it was still dark and spooky outside, and very cold. Dat ate hurriedly and went out to start the fire in the stripping room at the tobacco shed. The room had to be heated.

The men had moved the dried tobacco down from the top of the barn to the damp cellar, where it hung until it became limp like rags. Then they brought it into the stripping room. Now it was ready for stripping, sizing and baling—a big job. Every child had to help.

"We'll do the dishes, Mam," said Beck.

"And let you go on out and start," said Bib.

"All right," said Mam. "But Beck, go and call Jonas. He's an old sleepyhead. No wonder—up so late last night." Mam smiled as if she was happy about it. Then she added, "Let the little ones sleep. You girls come out as soon as you are done here. I'll take the milk buckets with me."

She put on her warm coat, and tied a kerchief around her head. She went into the kettle house, took the buckets on her arm and stepped out on the porch.

Shoo-Fly picked up a dish towel and a dish. Suddenly she heard a clatter of buckets and a heavy thump and commotion.

"What's that?" asked Bib, her hands deep in dishwater.
"It's *Mam!*"

Shoo-Fly ran out through the kettle house, towel and dish still in her hand. The walk was icy. All she could see in the darkness was Mam crawling on the walk on her hands and knees. All she could hear was her mother's moaning. The buckets had flown through the air and landed in the yard.

"Call Dat!" cried Mam, in a frightened voice. "Call Dat! I'm dying! Call Dat! Bring him *quick!*"

Shoo-Fly had no time to think, she was terrified. Dropping dish and towel she tried to move, but her feet were sticks of wood. Dat was in the stripping room and the tobacco shed was clear across the barnyard. She stepped off the porch and fell into a tub that stood at the base of a frozen spouting. There was water

in the tub, but she got herself out after scraping her arm against the porch post. She ran through the gate and ducked under the barbed-wire fence. She kept on running, screaming at the top of her voice. She ran with vigor and with all the strength she could summon, the dog Pretzel at her heels.

"Oh, Dat! Please come! Mam hurt herself and says she's dying! Dat, come quick! Mam's dying!"

Dat came rushing out of the darkness, alarmed by her cries.

"Where?" he shouted. "Where is she?"

"Kettle house!" answered Shoo-Fly.

It was barely 6 A.M. and still dark. Dat came rushing along the icy walk and not seeing the tub of water by the porch, went smack into it too. He jumped out quickly and made for the door of the kettle house. Shoo-Fly crawled under the barbed-wire fence on her way back and was so excited she did not notice where she was going. Again she stumbled over the tub and skinned her leg the second time.

Where was Mam?

She was not crawling on the sidewalk now. Beck and Bib had helped her indoors and she was lying on the kitchen couch. Her clothes were soaked and the girls were taking them off. They had taken off her coat and the kerchief from her head.

"Ach, my side, my side!" groaned Mam. *"Ai-y-y,* the terrible pain in my side. I'm dying! I'm dying!"

Dat came over and put a pillow under Mam's head. He knelt by the couch and tried to soothe her. He gave her some pills to take. After a while the pain lessened. Mam stopped moaning and smiled.

"What happened, Rachel?" asked Dat.

"I fell into that pesky tub of water!" said Mam, smiling foolishly. "The walk was icy, I didn't see the tub, stumbled and fell right into it. The wooden handles hit me right here in my side . . . and gave me such a terrible pain, I thought I was dying. . . ."

"Is it better now?" asked Dat.

Mam sat up on the couch. *"Ach, ja,* so it is! It still hurts a little, but . . ." She looked at her husband and her eyes grew big with astonishment.

"Why, *you're* soaked too!" she exclaimed. "Your pants are dripping water all over the floor. . . . Look!"

It was true. Dat was standing in a puddle of water.

"I fell in the tub too!" he confessed, with a grin. "I was in such a hurry I didn't look where I was going." He looked and saw Shoo-Fly standing openmouthed, nearby.

"Susie, why didn't you tell me Mam fell in the tub?" he asked.

"Did Mam fall in?" cried Shoo-Fly. "I didn't know what had happened to her. I just saw her crawling on her hands and knees on the ice and heard her say she was dying . . ."

"Why do we have a tub of water sitting on the sidewalk?" growled Dat.

"I put it there to catch the water from the spouting," said Mam. She glanced at Shoo-Fly.

"Why, *you're* soaked too, Susie!" she cried.

They all looked at Shoo-Fly, Beck and Bib too. Now she was in for a good scolding, she supposed.

"Look how wet you are!" said Beck.

"And no shoes or stockings," said Bib. "You went outside like that?"

"No coat, and nothing on your head either," said Beck.

Shoo-Fly was ashamed to admit it. "I didn't have time to think of putting on wraps." She went on in a very small voice. "I fell in the tub *twice*, going out and coming back. I was so excited and trying to hurry so, I never even saw it."

The water was dripping in puddles from her skirt.

"And you had no coat on and your feet and head bare," said Mam.

"I didn't have time . . ." said Shoo-Fly.

"I'll say she didn't," said Beck.

"She ran like a streak of lightning," said Bib.

They were not scolding. They spoke with real concern.

Shoo-Fly raised her arm, pulled the sleeve back and looked at it. It was all skinned and bruised. It began to sting. She lifted her skirt and looked at her bare leg. It was skinned and bruised.

Her hurts were not funny, but everybody laughed.

"What a bunch of ninnies we all are!" shouted Dat. "Three of us all falling in the same tub!"

"A fine way to get an early start at stripping tobacco!" cried Mam, getting up from the couch.

"How is your side now?" asked Dat, with a worried look. "Do you think you should get up so soon?"

"It was just a bump. The pain is all gone now," said Mam. "I guess I'm not going to die now after all. We'll get the tobacco stripped first. The Lord doesn't want me yet."

She got up, put her arm around Shoo-Fly's shoulder and spoke in a quiet voice. "The one that got hurt the most said the least. Come, girl, back to bed you go, and dry clothes for all of us."

"Oh, Mam!" cried Beck. "I forgot to tell you in all the excitement, Jonas isn't home yet. His bed is empty."

Shoo-Fly's face turned white. She began to shake all over. He was gone then. She should have warned them, even if it was a secret and she had promised not to tell. She should have warned them, because she was the only one who knew he was going. Now it was too late. Jonas was gone.

Dat said, "That boy not home yet? And it's six-thirty in the morning? He's making quite a night of it."

Mam looked at Dat. "He ought to be home by now. He shouldn't stay till daylight. He's pretty young, not sixteen yet."

Shoo-Fly tried to say, "He's gone to Canada, he told me he was going," but the words would not come.

All at once footsteps were heard outside, and the next minute in came Jonas, with a sheepish look on his face.

"What's this? Everybody waiting up for me?" he said with a laugh.

Ah! he had decided not to run away after all, not yet anyhow. Shoo-Fly was so glad to see him she felt like hugging him. But she stayed where she was and said nothing.

"What are you all standing around for—doing nothing?" cried Jonas. "Have you run out of *work* to do?"

There was tension in the air, but Bib broke it.

"We've been waiting up just for you," she said mischievously.

"We wanted to check on you and see how long you stay when you go to call on your girl friend."

"Pretty late hours for little Mary Esh, don't you think, Jonas?" teased Beck. "She's only fifteen, she's not used to being up all night. Didn't you run out of conversation? What did you talk about—the tobacco crop?"

"*Ach,* now, you girls shut up!" growled Jonas. "I left there at twelve-thirty."

Dat saw that Jonas was embarrassed. He tried to change the subject. After all, the boy had to start stepping out sometime, and the sooner the better.

"Did you unhitch Skipper and put him back in his stall?" he asked.

"*Ach, ja,*" said Jonas. "Sure I did. Fed him too."

But Mam was not so easy. She wanted to know the whole story.

"What took you so long to get home then?" she asked.

Dat pricked up his ears and spoke too. "You didn't stop at a tavern, did you?" He went close to the boy and spoke sternly. "You haven't been drinking, have you?"

"*Ach,* no!" cried Jonas. "Don't get excited. I'll tell you. I'll tell you. . . . A person can't keep anything to himself in a family like this. I was driving home and everything was nice and quiet and Skipper was stepping along, eager to get back home. But up there in Honeybrook, I guess I turned the corner too short . . ."

"Did you wreck the buggy?" asked Dat sternly.

"I thought you knew how to handle Skipper," said Mam, anxiously.

"Wait a minute," said Jonas. "All I hit was a stop sign . . . and I broke the shaft on one side, so I couldn't drive any farther. I had to take time to think things over. I didn't want to leave the buggy there, out on the street, and I couldn't let Skipper go. So I had to figure out a way of getting both Skipper and the buggy home."

Beck and Bib and Mam and Dat all began to smile.

"What did you do?" asked Mam.

"The only thing I *could* do!" said Jonas. "I tied the horse to the back of the buggy and started to pull the buggy out of town . . ."

The others began to roar with laughter. Shoo-Fly laughed too. Jonas pulling the buggy with the horse behind—what a joke!

Jonas had to laugh himself. "I was glad it was night so nobody could see me. Don't you folks go telling it all over the district or I'll never hear the end of it!"

"What then?" asked Dat. "Go on with your story."

"First I thought I'd leave the buggy at an Amish farm along the way and ride Skipper home," said Jonas. "But when I got to the first one, Nathan Glick's, I knew it would only cause a lot of gossip, so I decided to go on to the next one. And when I got to the next one, I kept thinking about all the gossip and teasing, so I didn't leave it there either. I decided to go on home, so I pulled the horse and buggy the whole five miles!"

Now they laughed more than ever. The younger children got up and came running in. Then they had to tell Jonas about all the excitement of falling into the tub. They all laughed again. Mam said the pain in her side was completely gone now.

"Whew! I'm tired!" cried Jonas. "I left the buggy at the carriage shop, Dat. The right shaft will have to be replaced."

Dat did not scold. He thought Jonas had handled a difficult situation pretty well. The boy was showing signs of growing-up.

"A late start to the stripping room," said Mam. "You go on to bed, now, Jonas, and you too, Susie."

But Shoo-Fly did not want to go. She said she was not sleepy. She put on her shoes and stockings and went out to the stripping room to help with the tobacco.

The stripping room was nice and warm. Because there were so few windows gas lanterns hung on the wall and gave a cheerful light. The whole family worked together at a long bench.

Mam and Bib sorted out the leaves and began stripping them from the stalks. They had to hold the stem and pull the leaves

by hand. Beck, Rags, Shoo-Fly and the twins sorted the leaves
for size and laid them in piles. Dat and Uncle Chris tied and
bundled the leaves together in sheaves. Then they placed them
in baling boxes, which would be bound and wrapped, then
hauled to the warehouse in the spring. Tobacco was a depend-
able cash crop for the Amish farmers, but it meant long hard
work for all the family from one spring to the next, to achieve it.

They all chatted and talked and laughed. Sammy and Hayfork
played on the floor, tumbling over each other like puppies.
When the twins got tired, they stopped and played, too. But
Shoo-Fly kept on working.

Everybody was there but Jonas, who was upstairs in bed, sleeping off his night's adventure. Shoo-Fly felt better about him
now. He had only gone to see his girl friend. It wasn't Lydia

Zook, it was Mary Esh now. How many different girl friends would he have before he settled down and got married? A boy was not supposed to pay evening calls until he had a courting buggy of his own. Strange that Dat let him take Skipper and the family buggy, but Dad must know best. At least Jonas had not started for Canada yet. What could she do to keep him from going?

Beck and Bib began to sing their school songs, and pretty soon the others joined in. The work with the tobacco was monotonous but not hard. Each person had to do the same thing over and over, so it made the day seem very long.

In the afternoon Shoo-Fly began to nod. She was tired and her head ached. She began sniffling. She wished Grossmama was home in her comfortable warm house. If only Grossmama

were at home, she could slip out quietly and run over to see her. She was homesick for Grossmama. But Grossmama was still at the hospital. She was making good progress now, but nobody had said when she would be coming home.

A cold draft blew through the stripping room and Shoo-Fly shivered. Mam had put some salve on her scraped arms and legs, but they still hurt. Her throat felt sore again. She had chilled herself when she fell in the tub in the morning. She began to cough. She wasn't over her cold, after all.

Would the day never end?

Jonas came in later to take Dat's place, while Dat went to the carriage shop. Jonas was refreshed after a long sleep and felt very lively.

"What's all the hullaballoo about?" he cried.

"*Ach,* we were just singing . . ." said Beck.

"We've sung all the songs we know," said Bib.

"Have you tried 'Baby Bright Eyes'?" asked Jonas.

"No, sing it for us," said Beck.

"Where did you learn it?" asked Bib.

"Is that what you sing to Mary Esh?" asked Beck.

Jonas picked up a bunch of tobacco leaves and hit her on the head with it. "It's the latest radio hit," he said. "They sing it in the movie by that name."

"What do you know about movies?" asked Bib.

"More than you think!" cried Jonas.

Shoo-Fly heard him and her heart sank. Had he been going to the movies, too?

Then Mam spoke up. "Enough of this foolish talk," she said sternly. "Remember now. We don't go to movies, have radio or television, but we do have *fun!*"

"*Fun?*" cried Jonas, in a daring voice. "Is it *fun* to have to work all day long? These kids came out here before daylight this morning. They've been working all day long. Singing too, but working steadily without stopping. Look at them!"

The little boys and the twins were sitting curled up on the floor, tired and listless.

"Look there! Look at Shoo-Fly Girl!" cried Jonas.

They all looked at her. She was huddled against the wall, half lying on the bench, her head resting on her arms, too tired to move.

She opened her eyes and said, "I'm all right," then closed them again.

"Shoo-Fly! Little Shoo-Fly Girl!" Jonas went over and touched her forehead tenderly with his hand.

"This girl's sick," he said. "She's got fever, she's burning up. She ought to be in bed. I'm going to put her there."

The little ones got up and stood and stared.

For once Mam said nothing. Jonas was acting like a man, like the man he would be someday. He picked Shoo-Fly up in his arms and carried her into the house. He took her upstairs and put her to bed. The work in the stripping room went on while he was gone.

He came back and stopped for a moment at the door. He said tersely, "I'm going for the doctor."

CHAPTER X

New-Found Treasure

Jonas! Jonas! Where was Jonas? He did not come when she called. Shoo-Fly turned over and tried to sleep. But she was too hot and began to cough. She threw the covers off. It was time to get breakfast. She had to comb her own hair and it took a long time. She must not be late for school. Hayfork and Sammy had dirty faces. The twins were crying . . . She started to get up.

Then she saw it. The sideboard was falling over, with all the glass dishes on it. The stove was jumping. The potted plants were falling down from the window sill. Whose plants were they? Mam did not have geraniums in the house. Where did they come from? Where was she? She lay back on the pillows and had to cough again.

Jonas was gone now, he never came when she called. Shoo-Fly was too late. Why didn't she tell Dat that he was going? No— it was Grossmama who was gone. Why did she run away? How could they get along without Grossmama?

Jonas! Grossmama! She tried to call, but she could not. Her voice was hoarse and her throat hurt when she tried to talk. She coughed and coughed and it hurt her chest. *Go away, Punkin! Go away, Puddin!* The twins were jumping over her and she could not sleep. Everybody made so much noise. How could she sleep? Oh, to find a good hidey-hole where she could be alone . . .

Somebody piled chairs and rugs and heavy comforts on the bed. *Don't do that! Take them off!* She could not turn over, she was burning up. *Jonas, don't go away and be 'English.' Jonas, come and help me. . . .* Grossmama was hurt, she fell out of the buggy. I must go and help her. *Jonas, Jonas!* Shoo-Fly tried to get out of bed again. *Grossmama! Grossmama! Where are you?*

Nobody came. They had all gone away, they had all gone away and left her alone. She rested on the pillows, her eyes closed.

Then she felt a cool hand on her forehead. Her face was flushed and very hot. She felt a cool spoon on her lips. Then it was taken away. It was hard to swallow whatever it was.

"Go to sleep now, Suzanna," a kind voice said.

It was a man. She roused again.

Was it the Mystery Man from Massachusetts? No, it was a stranger. Was it Mr. Ferguson, who killed her crow? No, it was a stranger. She had never seen him before. An "English" man, without a beard. He sat there by her bed. He held her wrist in his hand. He kept saying, "Try to sleep, Suzanna." The big clock on the shelf was ticking noisily. Sometimes it struck the hour, but she could not remember what time it was. She dozed off to sleep and the man went away.

The next time she woke, Grossmama was there. Was it a dream, or was she really there? Quiet little, brisk little gray-haired Grossmama with her white prayer covering on her head. She brought broth and tried to get Shoo-Fly to taste it. But Shoo-Fly was not hungry. Nothing tasted good. She asked for Jonas, but Grossmama shook her head.

"You are too sick to see anybody," she said.

Shoo-Fly looked around. She was not in her bedroom, not in the kitchen at home. "Where am I?"

"You are at my house," said Grossmama. "We brought you here, so I could take care of you."

"Where is Aunt Suzanna?"

"Outside feeding the chickens."

"But I thought *you* were in the hospital," said Shoo-Fly.

"I'm well again," said Grossmama. "I've been home for two weeks. You've been sick a long time."

After she began to feel better, they talked at length.

"You caught that bad cold at corn-husking time," said Grossmama. "It started with a runny nose and headache, and ended with a cough. You got better and went back to school. But that day when they started stripping tobacco, you got worse. Jonas was the one who noticed that your cheeks were too pink and your eyes glazed with fever. He put you back to bed and went for the doctor, who said it was pneumonia. There was so much noise and confusion over at your house that I brought you here. Here you can have peace and quiet. Here I can take care of you. Your Mam has her hands full—all the others half sick too."

"But I thought you got hurt and broke your ribs," said Shoo-Fly.

"*Ach*, that was nothing!" said Grossmama. "Only a little spill. God wasn't ready for me yet. He sent me home to take care of you."

"But the buggy—I saw it smashed to bits!" said Shoo-Fly.

"*Ach, ja*," said Grossmama, with a twinkle in her eye. "That old cheese crate will make good kindling wood! I'll soon have a better one. Rufus is making it already."

She cackled with glee. Grossmama took life as it came. She was always ready for anything.

"But Jonas—I want to see Jonas," said Shoo-Fly.

"Jonas is not here now," said Grossmama.

"I want to see him, I want to see him," said Shoo-Fly.

"You have been calling him all the time you were sick and delirious," said Grossmama. "He came to see you, but you didn't know him, you were too sick to recognize him. You got all of us mixed up."

"I want to see Jonas," said Shoo-Fly.

"Jonas is away now. . . ."

Shoo-Fly began to cry. "Why did you let him go away? Why did you *let* him?"

"Try to sleep now," said Grossmama. "You've been talking too much. You are all tired out. The doctor said you need rest."

She tried to get used to the fact that Jonas was gone. If only she had told Dat that he was going to Canada with Bill Ferguson, Dat would have stopped it. Days went by with Jonas gone, then one day he appeared. Shoo-Fly was sitting up in her bed when he came to see her.

"Hi, Shoo-Fly!" he said. "Been shooin' any flies lately?"

She looked at him in astonishment.

"They said you were gone."

"I was," he said, "but I came back."

"You went to Canada?" she asked.

"*Ach,* no! Of course not," said Jonas. "That was just a crazy idea."

"Did Bill go?"

"No," said Jonas. "That was all just talk. We had to let off steam. We talked of a hundred things we'd *like* to do. That don't mean we *did* them."

"Where did you go then?" asked Shoo-Fly.

"I had to go to Westchester to order new shafts and wheels for Dat. I went on the bus—*jeepers!* it was wonderful! Dat says he's going to give me more responsibility and later on take me into partnership. I won't be a farmer but a carriage maker like Dat!"

"But you said you hated being Amish and . . ."

"Yes, well, there were some things about it that bothered me," said Jonas. "I'm sorry I worried you so. What do you think? As soon as Dat gets a new buggy made for Grossmama, he's going to build one for me. And every week now, we go to the Horse Sale, looking for a horse."

Shoo-Fly smiled. "Grossmama says you'll want a pretty three-year-old, a pacer."

"*Ja,* that's what we're looking for."

"Who's your girl friend now, Jonas?" teased Shoo-Fly. "Is it still Mary Esh, or did you go back to Lydia Zook again? Are you letting your beard grow yet?"

Jonas turned red in the face. "I'm not sixteen yet," he said.

After all, Jonas was still at home. He wouldn't go away until he was old enough to be married and settle down. Shoo-Fly breathed a sigh of relief. One day there would be a fine wedding. . . .

The "English" man who had sat by Shoo-Fly's bed turned out to be the doctor. Then another man came and sat by her bed too, a man who was not afraid of germs. He was the same old Mystery Man from Massachusetts. Why didn't he go back to Massachusetts and stay there?

But she could not be mad at him this time. He brought her a bunch of red roses and two books to read, he brought the little ones coloring books and crayons.

He stayed and talked all evening. He talked to Grossmama and Aunt Suzanna, and to Dat and Mam, who came in for a while. Jonas was there and listened to every word.

He told about his sons who had wasted his money and wrecked the cars he gave them, and were always getting into trouble. He said his wife and children had left him and now he had no family at all. He said he had nothing more to live for. That was why he had bought his riding horse with Dat's help and taken up horseback riding—to forget his troubles.

Jonas sat on the edge of his chair and listened to the man's words. Shoo-Fly watched him anxiously. Was this the world Jonas wanted to run off to?

"I read about the plain people," the man said. "So I came to see them for myself. I am a different person when I come here. . . . I wish I could begin my life all over again."

"What do you like about the Amish?" asked Dat.

"You plain people have got something," the man said. "Something that makes the rest of us think. You've stayed close to the soil, close to God. Your self-denial, your resistance to temptation, your ability to get your living from the soil without the help of machinery, your love of good hard work, your ideals . . . these things appeal to me.

"I come down here to leave all the worries of my business and my worldly affairs behind. I've traveled all over the country and this is the only place where I am able to find peace and contentment. That's why I come so often. I love the plain people and all that they stand for."

Jonas listened openmouthed.

For the first time he realized his heritage and the value of it. Instead of bringing worldly temptation to the boy, the Massachusetts man had brought him satisfaction with his own way of life. His restlessness, an inevitable part of growing up, was gone now. He could be Amish wholeheartedly and follow in the ways of his fathers.

A great peace came over him.

After the man left, Jonas talked to Shoo-Fly again.

"That man told how his sons were so rich they had everything.

I thought I wanted to be like them. Then before I knew it, he turned around and showed me how lucky I am to be born Amish. So I guess I'll just stay that way."

Shoo-Fly smiled. The old Jonas was back again.

Every day now Shoo-Fly got up for a while. She took short walks, then went back to bed again. The doctor said she could return to school before long. The twins brought letters from all the school children, telling her to hurry up and get well. They brought her books and she studied awhile every day. Gradually she grew stronger.

One day she went home and sat down to watch Mam at her sewing. Her own new dress was done now and hanging on the wall. She would wear it the next time she went to meeting.

A brisk knock at the door and Mrs. Ferguson came bustling in, acting not like a neighbor but like a stranger. Her green car was out in the barnyard. The woman looked grim and angry. What could possibly be wrong?

"Won't you sit down, Mrs. Ferguson?" asked Mam politely. "Try this chair." She pushed the tulip rocker forward. "My Grossmama Yoder gave me this chair when I married."

"No, thank you," said Mrs. Ferguson coldly. "I don't want to sit. I can't stay long."

"Why, Mrs. Ferguson!" cried Mam. "What is the trouble? Can I help you?"

Mam went toward her, but she held up her hand.

"Don't come near me!" she cried.

"Why, what have I done?" asked Mam.

"It's hard to say," said Mrs. Ferguson, "but I thought we might as well get to the bottom of it."

"To the bottom of what?" cried Mam.

Mrs. Ferguson talked fast, her words came pouring out once she got started.

"I guess we're just as good as you are," she said. "You needn't think you're so holy just because your men grow beards and you women wear little white caps and bonnets, and you get your chairs from your grandparents instead of buying new ones in the store! *We* go to church and *we* listen to the preacher and *we* believe in the Bible too! What's more we try to do what's right. And even if we've got curtains and fancy clothes and television and automobiles, it doesn't mean we are wicked."

Mam took a deep breath. "Nobody said you were!"

"But some people act as if we are too 'fancy' and being 'plain' is the only way to get to heaven!" Mrs. Ferguson went on. "Our preacher said we're not committing any sin at all, and to just go on doing what we are taught is right."

"Of course," said Mam. "You've got as good a right . . . we all live in America . . . and here we can worship according to the dictates of our own conscience. That's why the Amish came and are still here."

But Mrs. Ferguson was not satisfied. She had other grievances.

"You keep on calling us 'English' and we're as German, I mean American, as you are. My parents came from Germany, but were not 'Dutch' or 'Amish'—just good Americans."

"We don't mean you came from England," said Mam, "just that you speak English."

"We were so sorry to hear about Grandma Fisher's accident," Mrs. Ferguson continued, "but what could we do about it? And even if my husband did shoot the pet crow, that was an accident too. We never even knew Suzanna had one for a pet, and we never dreamed she would get so sick . . ." Mrs. Ferguson began to cry. The tears ran down her face.

"It wasn't your fault," said Mam. "No one blamed you."

"We tried so hard to be friendly, but everything we did was wrong . . . and killing that crow was the last straw, Suzanna was so fond of it. . . . We wanted you to *like* us . . ."

The next minute the women were in each other's arms, crying.

"Oh, I wish we could be friends," said Mrs. Ferguson, sobbing.

"The Bible says we should love our neighbors as ourselves," said Mam. "I haven't done my part, but from now on I will."

Shoo-Fly had been looking on and listening. Now she could wait no longer. She ran to Mrs. Ferguson and put her arms around her.

"Don't you cry about the crow, Mrs. Ferguson," she said. "You couldn't help it. Don't cry, I love you, and I love Betty, too. And Jonas returned Bill's radio a long time ago, he told me so."

Mrs. Ferguson held her close and dried her eyes. "Oh, Suzanna, to see you up and dressed. Now you'll soon be well again. Betty missed you so at school. And she wants you to come over and stay all night soon, will you?"

Shoo-Fly promised to come.

"We'd like you to stay and eat with us, Mrs. Ferguson," said Mam. "Supper will soon be ready."

"Call me Dolly," said Mrs. Ferguson.

"And my name is Rachel," said Mam.

"My family will think I'm lost, Rachel," said Mrs. Ferguson, "but I guess they can get along without me for once."

Before she left, she said, "Sometime I want to learn how to make shoo-fly pie. I tried it once and it turned out terrible."

"Suzanna can show you how, Dolly," said Mam.

"They call me Shoo-Fly Girl because I bake such good shoo-fly pies," said Shoo-Fly.

One day Jonas took Shoo-Fly for a walk.

"I've got something to show you," he said.

They wrapped up warmly because the day was cold. A light coating of snow covered the earth.

"I saw a squirrel go into his hole in a tree down by the creek," Jonas went on. "I was curious to see how many nuts he had gathered for the winter. So I put my hand in and what do you suppose I found?"

"Tell me," said Shoo-Fly.

"I'll show you, instead," said Jonas.

They went to the tree. Jonas boosted Shoo-Fly up, so she could reach into the hole. She reached in and brought out one treasure after another. First Mam's lost scissors and Beck's lost thimble, then a dried chicken bone and bits of broken china that the twins used for play dishes. A handful of caps from ginger ale bottles, clothespins, some brightly colored marbles and shiny stones, and last of all the *Super 40 Chromatic* harmonica!

"I know!" cried Shoo-Fly. "It was not a squirrel at all. It was Jackie, my pet crow. This was his hidey-hole!"

"But the harmonica . . ." began Jonas.

"*Ach,* now, I hate to tell you," said Shoo-Fly. "But that night when you wouldn't take it, I was so disappointed, I threw it away. I tried to throw it in the creek, so I would never see it again."

"I was a beast," said Jonas, "to treat you like that."

"But Jackie found it and put it in his hidey-hole," said Shoo-Fly, smiling. "Look! It's as good as new."

"Crows love to hide shiny things," said Jonas.

"Jackie tucked all these things away and left them for me, for

keepsakes!" Shoo-Fly gathered them up in her apron. Her old pet, the crow, had given her back his treasures. She felt better now over her loss.

When they got back to the house, supper was ready. It was good to be able to come to the table and eat with the family again. They were waiting for her and Jonas. They slid in on their benches, bowed their heads and prayed prayers of thanksgiving.

The meal was good. Beck and Bib had cooked it all, while the twins had set the table. Goose filling and lima beans, red-beet eggs, noodles and scalloped potatoes, chow-chow and pepper cabbage, applesauce and grape mush, cornstarch pudding and canned peaches, but no shoo-fly pie. That was saved for breakfast.

After the cows were milked and the evening chores done, they all sat in the kitchen and talked. Grossmama and Aunt Suzanna came over. Grossmama sat in the tulip rocker and held the twins on her lap. Aunt Suzanna held Sammy until he fell asleep.

Shoo-Fly spread all the crow's treasures out on the table. Everybody laughed when they saw what the naughty crow had hoarded.

Jonas picked up the harmonica and began to play. First he played "Mary Had a Little Lamb," then "Coming Round the Mountain," while everybody sang. One happy song followed another.

Then Mam asked for her turn, and took the harmonica. She surprised everybody by playing "Home, Sweet Home."

After that, it was foot-washing time—time for bed.

Home was a good place after all. Home was peace and love.

Dat

The Twins

Henry
Hayfork

Jonas

Rags
Reuben

Shoo-Fly
Susanna